Andrea,
It's been a pleasure meeting you.
Thank you and God bless.

Bukola
1/13/14

IMPRISONED:

The Travails of a Trafficked Victim

BUKOLA ORIOLA

D1279606

... Towards ending human trafficking and domestic abuse among immigrants in the United States.

All rights reserved. This document cannot be published, used as a screen play in any other form in whole or part without written permission from the publisher.

IMPRISONED: The Travails of a Trafficked Victim

Printed in the United States

© 2009, by Bukola Oriola

ISBN: 978-0-615-32880-5

Revised, October 2012

Bukola Publishing (Bukola Braiding & Beauty Supply)

1628 County Highway 10 #210

Spring Lake Park MN 55432

763-433-9454

Websites:

www.bukolabraiding.com

www.imprisonedshow.com

Emails:

info@bukolabraiding.com

info@imprisonedshow.com

Cover design illustrator: Azeez Ozi Sanni

DEDICATION

This book is dedicated to God Almighty who restored my life, having gone through the hell of being trafficked and abused, my son, Samuel, who is my consolation, and all women who have gone through, or lost their lives, as a result of domestic abuse and human trafficking.

Imprisoned: The Travails of a Trafficked Victim

CONTENTS

ACKNOWLEDGEMENTS

First of all, I would like to give all the glory to God for granting me the privilege of writing this book. I thank Him for his grace that has kept me till now. I was dead but He gave my life back to me. I would also use this opportunity to thank all those who stood by me in my trying times.

Lori, I am grateful for showing me the way out of my dilemma by referring me to the battered women shelter, where my son and I were saved, especially, from the winter cold. You also visited us at the shelter and brought us Christmas gifts. You did not only do your work with dedication, but also love and care. You followed up with us and acted like that angel God sent to keep an eye on us to ensure we were doing fine.

My shelter advocate, Laura is the best I could have had. I couldn't have asked for more. She worked with me all the way through it all. She is such a good listener and always willing to help. She tried her best to ensure our stay at the shelter was enjoyable for us. Other staff members were also of immense help to us - Camille, Marie, Shawn, Denice, Sarah, Jen, Mo, Betty, Heidi, Lori, Barb, Kathy, Jenny, Rose, Luz and everyone that was there to help us. Becki, my mother's look alike. She both resembled and acted like her. When she heard my story, she thought that the domestic abuse class for refugee and immigrant women would be ideal for me. She was right. I learned a lot attending the class and became more aware of my surroundings and situation.

Until then, I did not know that for two years, I was a victim of domestic abuse and human trafficking. I got my life back and regained my freedom. Through the class, an attorney was assigned to me and my case was presented to the United States Citizenship and Immigration Service (USCIS).

I also want to say a big thank you to Laurel of the Elim Transitional Housing, my therapist at the Central Center for Family Resources, now Lee Carlson Center for Mental Health and Well-Being, Kathrine, who was encouraging and listening to me and Judith for the sexual assault support group. I am grateful to Erika, my case worker at the Anoka County and Mr. Sherrif, who is like a father to me. I owe Bri more than a million thanks. You are a life saver. Your encouragement and support gave me the strength to go on. I am grateful I worked with my attorney, Salima, who is such a professional that does her job with absolute dedication and to Civil Society for providing the legal support.

Acknowledgements

My father, Oriola Ogunmola and siblings, Abayomi, Abolaji, Olanrewaju, Olumide and Anuoluwapo are so important to me. They were there for me, even though, they were million miles away. Their prayers and calls made it feel like they were closer than one mile.

And, I want to use this opportunity to thank God that my father passed away on February 17, 2009 knowing that I have been saved from the torture and hopelessness I suffered, as a result of domestic abuse and human trafficking in the hands of my husband. Daddy, may your soul rest in perfect peace. If indeed, the dead see one another, say hello to my mother, Adeshola, your wife. I am grateful to Evangelist Amusan for your prayers and all the ministers of God that prayed along with you for me. I am also thankful to Bishop David Oyedepo, whose teachings reinforced my faith in the face of death and Pastor and Mrs. Ayesu, whose ministrations strengthened me in my time of need. Saying "thank you" to Shamera is an understatement. I don't have the right words to express my gratitude. You are a friend that "sticketh more than a brother." I am very grateful to you and your family for being there. You touched the deepest part of my heart by showing me true and great love. On behalf of Samuel, also, I say a very big thank you. My gratitude goes to Mr. Liquenda, who supported Shamera to help us.

I appreciate Roseline and Samuel Ejembi's support through emails and phone calls, including the Agunbiade's, Oshinuga's, Jibunor's, Mrs. Ajose, Gbadamosi, Adegbenro and Enwesi. Heartfelt gratitude goes to all my clients at Bukola Braiding & Beauty Supply, especially those who went out of their way to give me rides to and from the shop, sometimes, in the heap of snow. I knew it was not easy but they were relentless in their giving.

I would also like to thank those who worked with me to get this book published. My profound gratitude goes to Prof. Joseph Mbele of St.Olaf College, Northfield, Minnesota, who showed me how to get my book published, otherwise, it would have been another Word Document on my computer. It would have not been able to give the message of hope to the hopeless. God bless you sir. I am grateful to the illustrator, Azeez Ozi Sanni and his editor, Mr. Lekan Otunfodunrin. I also want to thank my first editor, Mr. Sunny Areh, and several other people, who have been of immense help to Samuel and me.

FOREWORD

Ever since I met Bukola Oriola when we both worked as Journalists in 2003, we have remained best of friends. We each reported education issues for our different media houses. She left Nigeria to cover the 2005 World Summit, which was held in New York.

Bukola agreed to stay back in the United States with her husband after much pleading from him. She had married him during a traditional ceremony in Nigeria before her journey. While in Nigeria, Bukola's intelligence, love and passion for the journalism profession was tremendous and this earned her many awards and admiration of her colleagues.

This book, *IMPRISONED: The Travails of a Trafficked Victim* is a true life story of the writer. It is an insightful revelation of what she and by extension, many others go through at the hands of their so-called spouses when living abroad. The book is both educational and informative, especially, for those who are going through a similar situation not knowing when and how to come out of it. The message is: There is hope and a way out for such people. I hereby recommend it to embassies, immigration department of all countries, schools and everyone traveling out of their country for marital or any other legal reason. It is a must read for all.

Rose Ejembi

Senior Correspondent

The Sun Publishing Limited

Lagos, Nigeria

PREFACE

Human trafficking is when a person is here in the United States as a result of force, fraud or coercion for the purpose of being subjected to involuntary servitude, forced labor, debt bondage, slavery or commercial sex exploitation. Force includes physical abuse of the victim while fraud may be luring someone through false offers of employment or marriage. Coercion on the other hand, means threat to the victim, or her family, debt bondage and psychological abuse.

This book, however, is destined to be an eye opener about the reality of domestic abuse and human trafficking, most especially, among immigrants now living in the United States. Even though there is domestic abuse in the African country, Nigeria, where I was born, it is not taken as a serious issue that should be addressed as it is in the United States.

Family takes more preference in Nigeria about family issues than the law. So, family members always intervene whenever something is amiss in a marriage. Maltreatment from one spouse to the other among the immigrants here in the United States, is therefore, common, especially when there is no family member to intervene.

The shocking aspect, however, is that, spouse who joined the one who is already a resident, or had naturalized as an American citizen, becomes a slave. In essence, the American citizen or resident was only looking for a victim that he would traffic into the United States, pretending to be a spouse. The victim is then turned into his slave for use as a material for his personal gain rather than a relationship of love. It is sad to note that this happens without anyone being suspicious - the victim or family members from their country of origin.

I therefore, hope to use this book to educate and reveal what happens among immigrants in the United States, in terms of domestic abuse and human trafficking through my own personal experience. I am doing this to educate other women who are either presently living in such a situation, or might find themselves in the same scenario. They need to know that life is not a bed of roses and that coming to America does not necessarily mean upgrading ones status. For me, I lost my status, career, self esteem and it was just a thin line that kept me wavering between life and death. I almost lost my life in the process. I suffered isolation for two years. I could not go wherever or whenever I wanted. I was at the mercy of my husband who took me whenever he felt it was necessary, or, on his own condition, and sometimes, for sex. I suffered throughout my pregnancy period. I could not eat whatever I craved. And, sometimes, I was at home in pain with little or no help. He pretended to care for me when others were around. When I worked, he took most of my money leaving me with virtually nothing to survive upon. It was a situation of a slave at the beck and call of her master. It could be described as the Israelites in the hands of Pharaoh and the Egyptians.

Therefore, I implore all victims to be conscious of the fact that there is help out there. There are shelters for battered women. There is immigration help too because abusive men and slave masters always use immigration as a weapon against their victims. You would not be deported if the United States Citizenship and Immigration Service (USCIS) found out that you have been abused and enslaved of a truth by a United States citizen or permanent resident. So, please, I beg, don't waste away at a man's hands, or worse still, lose your life. Go for help.

I also want to use this opportunity to encourage survivors to stop living like victims. Please, go for mental health therapy. It helped me. I believe it would help a lot of women who have gone through hardship in the hands of men. You do not only need legal status, but also your total health. As this book opens the eyes of many to be aware of their surroundings and the slavery going on around the world in recent times, I urge those who need help to speak out.

Readers should take note that the book is written in plain language and there are uses of words like the private part in it. Therefore, it contains adult content.

Due to privacy issue, some names have been changed, but, like I mentioned in the beginning of this message, it is a true life story and I hope that many would take advantage of my experience to seek for help.

Chapter 1

Deportation Or Death: The Ultimate Choice

When I walked through the door into the Alexandra House, the battered women shelter, I thought it was the end for me. I never imagined that I could leave that place into my own home. I thought two things could happen; it was either deportation or death. I could feel death; I was just a walking corpse. But, I did not want to lose my son. I kept thinking about who I could trust, to leave him with, at least, if I passed away. My mind was not settled. No one knew the agony I was going through.

I already lost touch with the world, so to speak. I could not even recognize myself in the mirror anymore. Whenever I looked in the mirror, I saw an old strange woman starring back at me, someone I had never met in my life. I touched my face and asked:

"Who is this?"

But I never got an answer of who that was. Jen one of the shelter advocates, did our intake in the playroom that afternoon of October 16, 2007. After relating my story to her in tears, she said:

"You are in the right place."

I did not know whether to believe it or not. The future was bleak. She took us into room one, the first room on the right side of the hallway. We took the lower part of the double bunk bed. I spread the bed sheet provided by Jen. She had taken us into the room with a cart of bed sheets, blankets, toiletries and basic needs we would require during our stay. She told me that residents were allowed to stay between 30 and 42 days, or more depending on each person's case.

Jen took me through the rules of the house. She also made me to understand that I would have chores - house job to do from the next day until I left the shelter. She said I would be assigned a primary advocate by morning the next day and that my advocate would be Laura. At the time we checked in, it was snack time and she asked if I would like to have snack. I refused, because I had no appetite for food or anything that went into the mouth except water.

There were two phone booths in the living area for us to make calls. On the wall were instructions on how to block the numbers whenever we wanted to make calls to those we did not want to find out where we were. I called a friend and told her where we were. When she finished from work, she came to pick Samuel, my son and I to eat out. She also took us to payless shoes where she bought us two pairs of shoes each. We stopped at Wal-Mart to buy socks and underwear.

We, however, had to return to the shelter before curfew, which was 9:30pm. I went to the shelter with just my documents and barely anything more, because, I did not want to raise suspicion of our escape from our matrimonial home.

Laura, resumed at 8 o'clock in the morning on Wednesday, October 17, 2007and invited me into one of the offices where I related my ordeal to her. She reassured me that, I was in the right place and that, I would regain my freedom - get an immigration status to remain and live in the United States without my husband. But again, I was overshadowed with doubts.

By Friday, I was taken to the legal office of the Alexandra House located near the Anoka County Government Court House in Anoka, Minnesota. They were going to file an Order For Protection (OFP) on my behalf and that of Samuel against my husband, Tade to keep him away from us. I met with Anne, a legal advocate who asked if I still wanted to go forward with an OFP, despite the risk involved: that is, my immigration status issue and being that my marriage with Tade was not documented.

According to her, if our marriage was documented, I would have been qualified to file for a status under the

Violence Against Women Act (VAWA). My life was more paramount on my mind. I wanted a safe place to stay alive to take care of my child, who was only 11 months old. So, I told her I would go ahead with the OFP.

I told my story while she typed. When I was finished, she said she would take it to the court for signature to make it legal. Then, my husband would be served after we might have been given a court date. Mind you, I was doing all that in fear. I could not tell everything that happened to me. I did not have the confidence to relate my entire story. I did not lie but I did not tell the whole story. I was going through all that without the confidence that I was actually with those who have my best interest at heart. I had been in a situation where those who were supposed to be for me had always betrayed me by blaming me for the pain I suffered in the hands of my slave master.

Our first court appearance was on Monday, October 29, 2007. I had a pro-bono lawyer through Alexandra House who represented me in court. I went in company of Anne and Kristin. They also accompanied another lady who was filing an OFP through them. When we got to court, however, Tade sought for continuance. He wanted to be represented by an attorney, so the hearing was adjourned for two weeks.

Meanwhile, my father had called from home in Nigeria to find out what was wrong. He told me that Tade's sister, who also lived in Nigeria, had called to harass him about the OFP that I filed in court. My father told me she called to advise him to tell me to withdraw the OFP against Tade because he feared deportation. But I told my father that I could not do so, because, I could no longer bear the suffering meted on me and Samuel. I also made him to understand that Tade had tried to put me in trouble with the law through threats, and, by calling the police to make false allegations against me. So, I needed to seek safety for my sake and that of the baby.

Imprisoned: The Travails of a Trafficked Victim

Chapter 2

My Son: My Consolation

As we continued to attend court hearings, my heart bled. I was so afraid that I did not know what to expect. Even though, there were shelter advocates from the legal office of the Alexandra House supporting me by going to court with me, I felt so lonely, cold and dead.

Becki, one of the advocates at Alexandra House was there for me too. She was in court as a witness, as I was afraid that Samuel might be taken away from me. His father had presented me as mentally incapable to take care of him. But he was all I had. He was my consolation for the agony I went through, so he was all that I could hold on to for life support. Despite the fact that I felt like a walking corpse, I held on to him for support and inner strength. Many a times, I held him close to my chest. And, several nights, I just hugged him tightly on our single bunk bed and cry bitterly. The saliva in my mouth tasted stale and bitter. I drank my own tears like water and my nose dripped like that of Pavlov's dog.

I was told that my case was a complicated one. But on December 10, 2007, in Judge Hayse's court room, the judgments were passed. My husband had also filed an OFP against me with false police reports saying that I threatened to kill him. He had lied to the police officers that I was his "girlfriend." After our testimonies and cross examinations, however, the judge dismissed his case, saying, he was only doing tit for tat, as I had filed an OFP on behalf of myself and my son against him first. Judge Hayse dismissed my case too due to lack of evidence.

I had no witness on the allegations I had against my husband. Those who knew what was going on would not show up in court or write an affidavit to support my testimony. In fact, I was not happy with the way my attorney handled my case. I believed she did not take it seriously. She had been trying to negotiate with Tade and his attorney and Tade had offered to change my immigration status as his wife which I had rejected. I was not fighting for immigration status but my life. I did not want to be with him anymore. I had suffered too much at his hands.   I returned to the shelter broken and dejected. I felt like justice did not take its course at the court house, partly, because I felt that my attorney did not do her homework properly. She barely cross examined the one who almost sent me to an early grave at my prime. She just treated the case like candy and cookies in the hands of toddlers.

At the shelter, I was made to understand that, I could still report the incident, especially, the rape aspect to the Crime Investigation Detective (CID). Becki, one of the shelter advocates called the Anoka Sheriff for the CID and detective Klossterman was sent to investigate the matter. The first time he visited the shelter for me was a Sunday but I was not there. I had gone to the shop. I will tell more about the shop, as that was where I worked later in this book. He left a message and promised to come back. On Monday, he called and we agreed that he should come over to the shelter that morning. I poured my heart to detective Klossterman while he wrote and recorded with a mini tape recorder. He asked for Tade's cell phone number and promised to call him to get his own side of the story.

I however received a letter from the Anoka County Attorney saying that a decision had been made not to "bring charges" against Tade. They thought that there was not enough evidence to prove my case. This decision, I believed, was due, largely to the fact that, I neither reported to the police nor went the hospital. It was also in that letter from the county attorney that I found out that Tade had made a second false police report against me while I was already seeking refuge at the shelter. He had alleged that I was threatening to kill and tarnish his record here in the

United States. It was part of his gimmick to taunt me with deportation.

I was further traumatized to know that Tade was head bent on ensuring that he molested me with the law, even, when I was already in transition to my freedom and sanity. I began to have nightmares and could not sleep at nights. At that point, I just prayed and hoped that the truth would prevail.

Chapter 3

My Career As A Journalist

I began my journalism career in 2000 at Common Interest Communications Nigeria Limited, publishers of National Interest Newspaper in Nigeria. I was very enthusiastic and dedicated to my job. In no time, I had mastered the ropes of the profession and was promoted to head the education desk. About two years later, National Interest Newspaper went through its dark period, and, due to non publication, it was not on the news stand.

Thereafter, I stayed at home for a while in pursuit of another job. Luck came my way one day when a colleague invited me to seek employment at Century Media Limited, publishers of NewAge Newspaper. I applied and was successful. In 2003, I joined the organization as a Reporter/Researcher and was also responsible for the education desk. Part of my duties were to ensure the publication of three pages of education weekly, edit stories of outstation correspondents (that is, those reporting for the organization from other parts of the country) for the education pages, plan the pages, in addition to sourcing and writing stories. In other words, I was responsible for the general aesthetics of the education pages.

As a staff member who took her job to heart, I went the extra mile to generate revenue for NewAge Newspaper through advertisements. I enjoyed my work, so I put in more effort to source for stories, especially, investigative stories. I took risks sometimes too. My first story for NewAge Newspaper was to write about best students in the West African Secondary School Certificate Examination (WASSCE) that was conducted in 2002.

I had to travel by boat, even though, I did not know how to swim and without wearing a life jacket on a boat that was paddled by a boy, who was about 10 years old. I embarked on this journey to reach one of the schools from which the students emerged to get my story. In fact, I plucked a water leaf from the river to show my editor, Steve, that I travelled across the river to reach the school which was located in a riverine area of Lagos State. As a journalist who did not want to lose her onions, I continued to generate investigative stories, source and write international stories, apply for national and international awards, including foreign fellowships.

I was given a consolation prize by one of the leading beverage companies in Nigeria, Cadbury Nigeria Plc during its 2003 national award for education reporters in Nigeria.

In 2005, however, I emerged as the national winner of the same award after submitting a story in which I investigated and revealed examination malpractice among students and invigilators during the 2004 WASSCE examination in Nigeria. Unfortunately, however, I was not there to receive the award. A colleague received it on my behalf. I also lost the chance to solicit for support from corporate organizations such as Cadbury Nigeria Plc, to curb examination malpractice in Nigeria.

I always strive to use the opportunity that I have to make a positive change in my area of specialization. Every week, I published a column titled *career guide*. This guide served as a resource tool to help prospective undergraduates. It shows them what job opportunities are available upon the completion of their higher education, while choosing their various discipline of study at the university, polytechnic or college of education in Nigeria.

I also applied for international awards including: The CNN Multichoice Award for African Journalists; The Bastiat Prize for Journalism and the United Nations Education, Scientific and Cultural organization (UNESCO) award for education reporters to raise my horizon as a journalist.

In 2004, I was selected to attend a six-week fellowship in Berlin, Germany, to study Multimedia and Online Journalism at the International Institute for

Journalism (IIJ). The program was sponsored and organized by Inwent, a ministry of the German government to support developing countries. At the training, I learned how to use the online and multimedia method to reach my audience. I planned to use the knowledge gained at the program to both reach my audience and also teach journalism students in Nigeria how to utilize the online media to pass their message across to their various audience.

At the end of the program, I was invited to one of the Nigerian polytechnics, Lagos State Polytechnic, Ikorodu, to give a presentation. This was a public event organized for the Mass Communication students of the school. I delivered a paper titled, *Multimedia and Online Journalism: The New Mode of News Delivery.*

Due to the positive response from the students at the event, I wrote a proposal to the German Embassy to join hands with NewAge newspaper to help journalism students in this area by organizing trainings in Nigeria for them.

All these dreams and aspirations were, however, cut short because of the story I am about to tell.

Chapter 4

The Traditional Marriage

Like I explained in the previous chapter, I produced three pages of education weekly. My deadlines were Sundays, because the pages would be published for Tuesdays. There is a first edition that must be ready by Mondays for the far Eastern and Northern part of the country. As a result, I spent most part of the day and nights at the office on Sundays to ensure the production of the education pages.

Sometimes, I finished around 10 o'clock at nights. At such times, I would spend the night at a friend's house that lived close to my office. The friend was a known person to my family. In fact, she and her husband became close to my family in 1996 when we started attending our church's house fellowship.   Their house was one of the locations designated by the church, and her husband was assigned as the minister of that location. We call her Aunty Nancy and her husband, Uncle Thomas. They have three children. I would sometimes go to their house to help with their children.

Our closeness could be described as that of a family rather than just friendship. When my mother passed away in 1998, they were both there for us. They became aunt and uncle to me and my siblings, and they too took us as their nieces and nephews. My father, also, took them like his younger siblings. It was a relationship of trust and love, so to speak, especially, with the church bringing us together.

At the time I became employed with Century Media Limited, Aunt Nancy had relocated to her father's house located in Ojuelegba, another city in Lagos which was close to my office when her husband travelled to the United States. I would spend the nights with her at Ojuelegba whenever I finish late at work on Sundays and could not go to my parent's house at Ipaja. It would have been too late for me to get public transportation to go home at that time of the night. Sometimes, when I was there, Uncle Thomas would call from the United States and his wife would tell him that I was around. I get to say hello to him on such occasions and ask how he was doing.

The night that I was introduced to my husband, Tade on the telephone happened to be one of such nights. Uncle Thomas had called and we exchanged pleasantries. I returned the phone to Aunty Nancy. While they were still on the phone, she turned to me to say that they would like to introduce me to a friend who resides in the United States, and was looking for a good wife.

According to her, they thought that I would be the ideal wife for Tade. She gave the phone to me and I asked Uncle Thomas about his friend that was mentioned to me by his wife. He then told me that his friend is a good person. He also acknowledged that they had known each other since childhood. Aunty Nancy convinced me that he was a born again Christian and that they would not encourage me into a relationship that would hurt me. I believed them. When we were about to sleep that night, the phone rang again and it was Tade. I was given the phone and we greeted. He told me he heard that I was a journalist and complimented me on my profession. I asked what he did for a living and he told me that he worked with a medical assembly company in Minnesota. He asked for my phone number and I gave it to him. Three days later, he called and we began to communicate on the phone. We exchanged photographs through emails, and would, sometimes, email each other back and forth. There were also a couple of times we chatted on yahoo messenger. We communicated mostly through telephone calls. He called almost every day. There were times we spent up to four or five hours on the phone. It got to the point that my siblings teased me about the long hours spent on the frequent phone calls from Tade. They usually said…

"…first half, second half"

As if it was during soccer matches.

Tade's phone calls became more frequent and I thought it best to tell my father about him. He proposed marriage. Then I realized that he was interested in pursuing a life-long relationship, or, at least, so I thought with me. I introduced him to my father on the telephone. He sent me an engagement ring through a friend of Uncle Thomas who came to Nigeria in 2004.

He told his family members about me. One of his sisters contacted me on the phone and we met when she invited me over to her house. I was also invited to the birthday party of his eldest sister's husband. I attended the party in company of two of my colleagues and friends, Nena and Rose. Tade, sometimes, spoke with my close friends and colleagues whenever he called and I was in their company. In October, 2004, he asked his family members to introduce themselves to my father and ask for my hand in marriage as the custom demands.

Traditional marriage in Nigeria, is an agreement between families of the bride and groom, therefore, they organize it in a way that is convenient for them. Once the parties involved agree, that is, the bride and groom, the families would go ahead and perform the rites. Sometimes, either the groom or bride is not present at the ceremony due to distance, and, at other times, both the groom and bride are not present. The family's agreements take preference in a traditional marriage. So, we conducted a traditional marriage during an introduction ceremony, where Tade was not present physically, but was represented by his families. The ceremony was presided over by Pastor Onatoye and it was at that ceremony that my father handed over my hand to Tade's family as his wife. Tade, who was supported by his cousin, Sean, however, called into the ceremony to introduce himself as the groom.

Imprisoned: The Travails of a Trafficked Victim

Chapter 5

My Journey To The United States

I continued to work as a journalist for NewAge newspaper hoping that Tade would come home to document our marriage at the Nigerian registry. This would enable me to join him as a married couple in the United States.

In September 2005, however, I entered the United States with an "I Class" visa, which enabled me to cover the United Nations 60th anniversary and General Assembly. My intention was to do my work, return home to Nigeria, and wait until Tade filed my immigration petition to join him. I gave my word to my employer and the consular officer, who interviewed me when I applied for the visa to return home after my assignment. I am also a law abiding citizen and a member of the Fourth Estate of the Realm. Journalists are referred to as members of the Fourth Estate of the Realm. I however applied as single because there was no documentation to prove that I was married. And, since I was only coming to the United States to work and return home, I did not think it was necessary for me to prove whether I was single or married to enable me do my job. While I was in New York, Tade's cousin, Sean invited me to visit his family in Connecticut for a weekend. I went to Connecticut by the Metro North train on a Saturday. Sean's wife, Silvia picked me up at the train station in Green Haven in company of her three children.

In the beginning, I felt like a part of Tade's family. When Sean arrived home from work, he welcomed me to their home and family at large. He received me as a new wife who had been added to their family folks. Silvia took me shopping and bought me gift items. She however, had already shopped for some clothes for me before I got there. According to her, she was able get the right size for me from the description of me given to her by her husband, as was told by Tade.

On Sunday, we went to church together. After church, I attended a birthday party with them. They drove me back to New York to resume at the United Nations on Monday to report for NewAge Newspaper. At New York, they met my Uncle and Aunt, Mr. and Mrs. Agunbiade, whom I was staying with during my time in New York to offset hotel cost. During my stay at the Agunbiades, Uncle Thomas and his friend, Pastor Mattis visited me. I was happy to see Uncle Thomas. I had not seen him for over two years. He was only home in Nigeria for a brief period of time when his third child was born in 2002.

When I finished my work at the United Nations, Tade bought me a flight ticket to visit him. I decided to visit him in Minnesota before returning to Nigeria because I had a flight ticket that covered me for two months. When I got to Minnesota, Tade received me warmly by throwing a welcome party for me in his home. I was introduced to some of his friends. He took me for sightseeing at various places like downtown Minneapolis and the Mall of America, the largest indoor mall in the United States.

We visited different stores where he shopped for me. I used the opportunity to buy gifts for my family, friends and his family. During this same period, my uncle, Tony, who lives in California invited me to visit with him and his family. Uncle Tony bought me a return ticket to California for a weekend.

Meanwhile, in Minnesota, I had covered the Nigerian Independence Day on October 1, 2005 for NewAge Newspaper. During my interaction with some of the participants, who were wondering if I was working for a media organization with a local newspaper here in Minnesota, I told them that I was only in the United States for an official assignment, and would be returning to Nigeria to continue my work as a journalist.

In Minnesota, I met Femi, his wife Kemi and their children. They had two kids while Kemi was pregnant and almost due for delivery. We were introduced to one another on the phone by Tade while I was still in Nigeria. They had come to visit me too because they lived not too far from his apartment.

Before I embarked on my journey to the United States, one of my co-workers, Cynthia, who worked in the accounting department of Century Media Limited became aware of my intention to travel for an assignment. I had taken my voucher to the department for my visa application fee when she found out. She asked if I could take some gift items to her sister, Josephine who also lived in Minnesota. When I was leaving for the United States, I agreed to help her deliver the gift items, and she gave me her sister's number.

When I arrived at New York, I called Josephine and told her that she would pick her gifts up at Tade's house, as the original plan was for Tade to visit me in New York. The plan changed, however, and he decided that I should come visit him in Minnesota. I was naive to suspect that something was not right. My aunt and her husband were not pleased with him not coming to visit me in New York. I had told them my husband intended to visit me while I was at the United Nations reporting. His excuse for not coming was that he incurred unexpected expenses which led to low funds in his account. By the time I finished reporting at the

United Nations, he had put his account in order and decided that I should visit him in Minnesota.

I called Josephine to let her know I would bring her gifts to Minnesota and have an opportunity to meet her in person. She came to Tade's resident to pick her gifts and then invited me to her daughter's birthday party, to be held in few a days. She lived in White Bear Lake, a suburb of St. Paul, Minnesota. Tade took me to the party at her house. Her daughter had turned seven and she had invited her friends from school to celebrate with her. There were few children at the party with their parents; overall it was a moderate party for a seven year old.

Tade and I continued to communicate with Josephine and she told me she would like to send some gift items back to her family in Nigeria when I was leaving. She packed a bag and gave me money to take it as an extra baggage at the airport. She had weighed the bag and brought the scale to Tade's house to show me that it was not over the 70 pounds airline requirement. Tade decided to travel with me to New York and also use the opportunity to visit Sean and his family. He had not seen him for over 15 years and had never met his family.

We arrived in New York on Friday, October 28, 2005 in the evening. From the airport, Sean's friend, who was a taxi driver picked us up and took us to my aunt's house. I introduced Tade to my aunt and her husband. During my visit to Minnesota I had left my bags at their house, since I would be leaving for Nigeria from there. They lived about 15 minutes from the JFK International airport. My aunt had prepared dinner for us. While I was in the kitchen with her serving dinner, she said that Tade took good care of me for the four weeks that I was with him. She said I had put on weight and was looking radiant. Her husband also had a chit-chat with him. When dinner was over, Tade decided that we should leave for Connecticut that night. We went to Manhattan to board the North Metro train which took one hour to reach Green Haven. Sean picked us up from the train station. They were very enthusiastic to see each other, and throughout the entire journey to Sean's house, they chatted none stop. When we arrived, Silvia as usual, had prepared dinner and set the guest room for us.

On Saturday, they took us around for Tade to see the city and the Yale University. They bought us birthday gifts because my birthday was October 30 and Tade's November 3. Tade had bought me a set of necklace and earring for my birthday shortly before we left Minnesota.
We had also bought gift items for Sean and his family which they were all happy to receive.

Meanwhile, Tade had been trying to talk me into staying with him, but I told him I needed to resume my work in Nigeria. Moreover, I came to the United States with a work visa and that he should come to Nigeria to register our marriage and file for me as his spouse. Sean began to beg me, also, on behalf of Tade not to return to Nigeria. According to him, Tade was growing old in age, and needed his wife with him so they could start a family. Tade had no children and his family members wanted him to have a family of his own.

When we were leaving, Silvia bought some wristwatches and took souvenirs from her brother's wedding that took place in Alabama some few weeks before then, and gave to me to help give her family members in Nigeria. Sean took us back to New York for Tade to return to Minnesota. He would need to resume work that night. I boarded the train from the airport to my aunt's apartment. But at my aunt's house, Tade's pleading continued on the phone. When he assured my aunt and her husband of taking care of me as his wife, they agreed that I should stay. He also promised to file my immigration petition to change my status by documenting our marriage here in the United States. After all the pleadings, I decided to stay. I called my father in Nigeria and told him of my decision to remain in the United States with my husband. He agreed because, he believed his relatives, that is, my aunt and her husband would make a good judgment.

Having decided to stay, my aunt helped me to cargo the items I had bought to take home, including the gifts I was supposed to deliver to Silvia and Josephine's family, as my flight to Nigeria was scheduled for November 2. Tade bought another ticket for me to return to Minnesota on November 9, 2005.

Chapter 6

Deceived Into Slavery

When I returned to Minnesota, Tade had purchased a new computer. He said I should tell my editor that I would continue to write for NewAge Newspaper here in the United States. I told my editor about the many opportunities that it could derive for the company by working from here, such as: writing about the Nigerians who reside in Minnesota and generating advertisements from the Nigerian business owners and other United States-based organizations with interest in Nigeria. My editor liked the idea and agreed.

Tade had also subscribed to Internet and Cable service provision for the house, which he said would be for my convenience. He told me that I would have to be patient as things would take shape one after the other. He was desperate to have a child with me but was very timid, as he had told me that his first marriage suffered due to the lack of children, and his former wife was against him 'testing' medication on her. According to him, after numerous unsuccessful attempts, they decided to see a medical doctor, who ran some tests and came back with the results that he had low sperm count. He was on testosterone 35% CRE prescribed by a medical doctor. I did not mind him using medication with me, as I could have been the one with a medical condition that needed medication to be corrected. In desperation to have a baby, Tade made several promises to me. But, of all the promises he had made, the one that stood out the most, because it was just so funny was…,

…"if you have a baby for me: Oh! My darling, I will buy you a Lexus jeep."

It was just empty promises. His family members also called and begged me to have a baby with their brother. They said he was getting old and needed to have his own child. I told them that it was in God's hands, and that we should hope and pray that God would give us a child. It was to the point that his friends were teasing him that he was impotent and could not impregnate a woman.

One morning during my prayers, I made a promise to God that if He gives me a son, I would give him back to Him, and his name would be called Samuel. I have my trust in God and always look up to him whenever I was in need or challenged. I knew this particular challenge would only take God. So, I used the Bible story on Hannah in the Book of First Samuel to pray and God answered the prayer. I missed my period the same month that I made that prayer.

When I told Tade that I was pregnant, he was happy, but little did I know that my frustration had just begun. His happiness was short lived. It appeared that all he wanted was to prove to himself, his family and friends that he could father a child and that his body had no problems. This was a *macho* thing since he wanted to prove his manhood. He received calls from his friends, the same ones that would tease him about his inability to impregnate a woman, telling him that he was now a man and welcoming him to the manhood club. Once I became pregnant, he lost all interest in me; his attitude changed so much towards me that I started to wonder:

"What happened to the man that I knew?"

He had become a different person and it was then, I realized that, I was only a vessel through which he could prove his manhood. Remember, when I decided to stay in the United States with my husband, he had promised to file my immigration petition to change my status as his wife. Months went by and nothing was done about it. Whenever I asked, he told me that he would do it. So, like a fool, I waited patiently. I was at home doing nothing and when I got tired of waiting on Tade to file my immigration petition, I resorted to hair braiding in the house. I was not used to idleness.

About the time I conceived, we were watching American Idol in the living room downstairs one evening when he went upstairs to get ready for work. He worked third shift with a casting company in Plymouth, Minnesota. We lived in a three bedroom Town-Home in Ramsey. At this time, we had relocated from the apartment we were living in Brooklyn Park, North-West suburb of Minneapolis to this Town-Home that he had purchased.

I heard a loud bang upstairs and asked what was wrong but did not hear a response from Tade. Out of curiosity, I decided to go and see what happened. To my shock, he was lying unconscious in the guest bathroom. The toilet bowl was filed with blood. I did not know what to do so I began to pray. I called his name and shouted… "…The blood of Jesus."

Luckily, he revived but could not recall how he went on the floor. I helped him into the shower to wash up, and then, helped him onto the bed to lie down. I asked him what to do and he told me to call one of his friends who lived close to our house to take us to the hospital. We ended up at Mercy hospital Emergency Room (ER) in Coon Rapids. Doctors confirmed that he was excreting blood. He had actually been excreting blood for two days but thought it was a coloring from the punch he had drunk. He was transferred to the Intensive Care Unit but nothing was found in the X-tray that was taken so he was discharged to go home after two days or so.

Few days after we got home, he farted and there was blood in his underwear. We went back to the hospital and a cat-scan was done. The result of the cat-scan showed that there was an unfamiliar tumor in his stomach. He was scheduled for surgery immediately. There were no available beds at Mercy Hospital. We were, therefore, transferred to Unity Hospital in Fridley. At Unity hospital, the surgeon who was scheduled for the surgery came and told us that he did not know what he would find in Tade's stomach. According to him, the tumor was very big and did not look familiar. The Chaplain came into the room to pray after the nurse in charge put us through some formalities with surgical patients. He was taken to the theatre at the lower part of the building. I waited anxiously in the waiting area, with two other people who had their loved ones on the surgical table. Four hours later, the surgeon came out to tell me that the surgery was a success. I felt relieved and was taken to his room on the third floor. At that time too, Uncle Thomas and his friend, who is a pastor here in Minnesota found that we were at the hospital, they were with me, including Femi and his family.

At the hospital, I suffered hunger. I was tired but had to stay strong for Tade. I fed on turkey sandwich to sustain myself and the fetus. Even though, I was there to support him, he never cared about my survival and that of the new baby I had just conceived. He blamed me for asking the nurses for food whenever we were alone. Luckily, Kemi brought me some cooked rice and chicken stew with gari (cassava grain). When the rice finished, I went to the cafeteria to make hot water in the microwave to make *eba*, a paste made with gari and eat with the chicken stew.

We spent more than a week at the hospital. The doctors had to monitor him to ensure he was healthy enough to go home. And, because, I did not know that we would not be able to go back home the day we rushed to the ER at Mercy Hospital, I did not take anything with me. As a result, I did not take my bath for three days and could not change my clothes, including my underwear. I was only able to use the hospital toothbrush and paste to clean my mouth. Femi had to come to the hospital one evening when he finished from work to take me home to clean up and change clothes. At home, I found $10 which I took with me to buy food, at least, to alleviate my hunger. But I was not too familiar with the food served at the cafeteria. So, one evening during the cold of winter, I was so hungry, I could literally feel the baby draining the little energy I had, I walked about one mile to a McDonalds restaurant from the hospital. To make it worse, I did not have adequate warm clothing and shoes on. I purchased a sandwich and then walked the mile back to the hospital. By the time I got there, the food was so cold that I could not eat it. My whole body was itching from frost bite. I suffered in silence, and in order not to be chastised by my husband, I pretended as if all was well. At that point, I knew I was living with an enemy. When we got home from the hospital, Tade continued to maltreat me. He never cared for me either in terms of food or clothing. I could not stand the maltreatment anymore and I wanted to go back home to Nigeria, but I had no money, not even to buy the ticket. I did not know how to go.

I begged him at a point to buy me a flight ticket to go back to Nigeria but he apologized, promising to change if I stayed, but that was just another of his manipulative, mind controlling tricks that he would play. I could not turn to my family for help either. My father could not afford my flight ticket. I called my friend, Rose to tell her what was wrong but because she did not know the extent to which I was suffering, she encouraged me to stay for the baby's sake.

I also found that he was a fraud. He would not file my immigration petition because he did not divorce his first wife legally. He only separated from her. According to him, he did not know her whereabouts and could not get her to sign the necessary document to proceed with the divorce. He put an advertisement in the newspaper promising to go ahead with the divorce but he never did. At some point, he went to the court house to get divorce forms but never took any action. I was trapped in the house like a prisoner. Worse still, I did not know how to drive. So, I did not know my way around. I stayed in the marriage and suffered. I could not talk to anybody as he had threatened that if I did, I would be in trouble with him and the law.

He registered me for prenatal visits to be able to see a gynecologist or midwife during my pregnancy. He told me under no circumstance should I identify him as the baby's father and if anybody asked, I should tell him or her that the father lived in Africa. Like a puppy at its master's mercy, I followed all his rules and regulations. He said that is how it is done here; otherwise, I would be in trouble.

Had it not been for medical assistance, I would not have been able to afford doctor's visit and prenatal appointments. My medical insurance provided me with car ride to my prenatal appointments. He refused to accompany me to child birth class. I went alone for the two days it took. I knew I would be on my own during labor and delivery. The thought of that scared me, so I started making enquiries for free childbirth doulas. Doulas are professionals, who give support to a woman during labor and delivery whenever there was nobody like family members or friends to support her. Tade, however, decided that he would go to labor and delivery with me.

During my pregnancy, I could not eat whatever I craved, because my husband would not provide it for me. We went to Brooklyn Park Cub Foods one day and I was craving bananas desperately and went to pick some up, he shouted at me saying:

"Where do you want to get money to buy bananas?"

I was embarrassed, as there were other shoppers around standing and staring. I told him that he did not have to shout at me like that. And, all he had to simply say was that there was not enough money to buy bananas.

At 10 weeks pregnant, on a Friday, I was uncomfortable and threw up the entire day. I called the nurse link health line at the hospital because I did not feel better even until the next morning around 2am. The nurse I spoke to advised me to go to the ER. I put the nurse on hold to go ask Tade if he could take me to the hospital. I was not confident enough to tell him to take me from fear that he might get upset. He was at home that morning because he does not work overnight on Fridays. His shift is from Sunday to Thursday nights. Luckily, he agreed and I went back to tell the nurse on the phone that I would be able to make it to the hospital. Still, he complained that I took a pillow with me. I had to explain that the nurse asked me to use it to support myself and sleep on my left side until I reached the hospital.

At 27 weeks pregnant, one night, I was having contractions. I did everything I could to feel better but nothing worked. I had to dial 911 for an ambulance to take me to the hospital since Tade had gone to work. By the time I got to the hospital, the contractions had subsided. I was however examined and was given sleeping medication. I was told to take it easy and not stress myself, as that was not healthy for the baby. But considering my dilemma, I knew it would not be easy for me. By morning, when Tade returned from work, he saw the hospital wrist band on my hand; he never bothered to ask what was wrong. Even when I called his attention to it, he still did not give a damn. When I went back to the clinic for my prenatal appointment, I asked the midwife why I was feeling contractions at home but not at the hospital, she told me it was because I felt safe at the hospital. At that time, I did not know I was having troubles with the pregnancy because of the hardship I was suffering at the hands of my husband.

I had had an argument with Tade before he left for work the night I was feeling the contraction. Even, neighbors attested to it. They said that they were afraid for me, as they knew Tade was maltreating me. But they could not intervene because I was not talking to anybody. One of our neighbors on the street, recounted to me several incidents that occurred at our house, including how they knew that he was neglecting the new born baby. I was told they were afraid that Tade had hurt me the day the paramedics came to pick me from home because they overheard our arguments before he left for work that night.

I was also told that they did not know that I could communicate well in English because I was not talking. I only waved to greet. But, that was where Tade had relegated me to. The neighbor also noted that her family was upset when the baby was crying uncontrollably one day as I tried to take care of him while braiding hair in our car garage, but my husband ignored him to go help another female neighbor do something at her house on the street. According to her, they concluded he was 'pimping' me to braid hair, because, I had started braiding hair barely one month after giving birth to our son.

During my pregnancy, however, Tade had taken me to one of his girlfriend's shop in Brooklyn Park to work as a maid under the guise that he was allowing me to go out. I had been complaining of getting stuck in the house. I was not used to that. I did not like idleness and wanted my freedom but Tade made it a nightmare for me each day of the two years that I lived with him.

At the lady's shop, I was supposedly a hair braider, but I would do other jobs such as selling her wares without pay. She told me also to pay her $125 a week (about $500) a month for braiding hair at a section she had set up as a salon, or share 50:50 of whatever I made braiding hair. I settled for 50:50 because I did not have $125 a week. There was little proceed from the venture which Tade took. He said he needed to use it to buy gas in the car. Moreover, he complained that he was not my driver to be taking me back and forth to the shop daily. Sometimes, I even had to spend the night at the lady's house because Tade would have to go to work if I was still working. It was very uncomfortable for me, especially with pregnancy. But, I had to keep going until the lady began to tell her clients that I was her maid who just came from Nigeria. She ordered me around the shop to do things for her to prove to her clients that I was her maid. When I complained to Tade he did not listen. Sometimes too, he would be discussing with the lady in the inner room at her shop and if I heard my name and asked what the matter was, they would both shout at me saying…,

…"go and sit down. Who is talking to you?"

I felt humiliated but I did not know what to do. I complained to my aunt in New York and she called him to find out what was wrong but he told all kinds of lies against me and denied ever maltreating me. When I could not take the humiliation at his girlfriend's shop anymore, I decided to stay at home and told him to do whatever he liked. He began to threaten me with the police and immigration, using the law against me. Each time I told a family member about it, he denied. They did not understand the truth of the matter. They were not living with us or close by. They could not come around to see things for themselves. He was such a manipulative person that they would only tell me to be patient with him not knowing the hardship that I was passing through.

My aunt and her husband sent me some maternity clothes when I complained to them of not having adequate clothing. The few clothes that I had would not fit anymore because of the protruding tummy. Even, his friend, pastor Ola had given me one of his shirts which he said was unisex. He was the one who also bought me a winter jacket when he visited us. I did not have a winter jacket and Tade would not buy one for me. He was also angry that I took the winter jacket that Pastor Ola bought for me. I felt sad that I had to beg for clothing during my first pregnancy with my husband. I was embarrassed that his friend noticed that I did not have enough and proper clothing to have offered me one of his shirts. It was hard for me to know that the same man who was desperate to have a child with me would treat me with disdain while I was pregnant with his child. It was unimaginable for me to believe that this was the same person who was making all kinds of promises before I conceived.

Imprisoned: The Travails of a Trafficked Victim

Chapter 7

A Prisoner In My Matrimonial Home

Whenever we went to church and we greeted African or African-American members, I let them know that I could braid hair. And, little by little, they were coming by calling to make appointments. My braiding jobs stood out and I got clients through referrals. I continued to braid hair at home, but the moment the client left, I had to hand the money over to my slave master. It was amazing how he knew the various hair styles and how much they cost.

He counted how many people came into the house to braid hair. Sometimes, he came into the room to chat with clients and would even offer drinks and food. After he left, some of my clients would make a comment saying: "Your husband is a wonderful man. You are lucky to have a man like that."
If only they knew the monster that lied within him, they would know I was very ill-fated. He looks gentle and quiet but he is the cruelest and most conniving person I have ever met in my life.

When my clients paid with check, he collected it to deposit in the bank, as I did not have a bank account. He would tell me that the check would clear in three to four days, but when I asked for the money, his response would be:

"You are not happy you are living in a free house in America, eating free food, using free light, using free phone, watching free TV and internet, you are asking for your money."

And, that is where the conversation would end. I continued to complain about needing my own account and I suppose he got fed up of my complaints and took me to a TCF bank at Cub Foods in Brooklyn Park to open a checking account. This was after the birth of our son. He knew either way, that, even with my own account, I would not be able to use it. He thought that if he did not take me to the bank, I would have no means of getting there. He had under minded my intelligence so much that he had no idea I too had a working brain. Each time I wanted to go to the bank I would make excuses that I needed to go to Cub Foods to get cereal or something for the baby. I use that opportunity to deposit the little money I was able to take back from my clients when they paid with cash. I was able achieve this aim by advising him to stay in the car with the baby. Then, I would run into the grocery store to put some money in my account pretending that I was going to buy rice cereal for our son. Sometimes, I asked my clients to pay part cash and part check. That way, I would give my 'pimp' the check portion.

Sometimes too, I would hide some of the checks my clients paid and deposit into my account whenever I was able to convince him that we needed something for the baby at the grocery store. After a while, 'pimp daddy' became suspicious that I wasn't giving him all the money, so he started keeping tabs of how many people came to get their hair braided. He would say:

..."Five people came today, where is the money."
He knew what styles they did and how much it cost, he would then ask for the money. He began to complain that I was hiding my money in my "vagina" instead of me giving my money to my husband like a true spoken 'pimp.' He knew there was no way I could go out alone.

In December 2006 he lost his full time job. Instead of going out to look for another job, he just sat around the house, waiting on me to give him my money. He warned me not to disclose to anyone that he had lost his job. Tade was so lackadaisical that he would have an interview for 10:00am but would get up from the bed to get ready at 9:45am, when the interview location was about 30 to 45 minutes away.

His gruesome attitude did not change, even, after the birth of the baby. I could not tell anyone, because each time I tried to tell someone about his unruly behavior, I was punished. Sometimes, my punishment would be denial of going out on a previously planned venture. He might have promised to take me out after complaining that I was tired of staying at home for probably two weeks without going out. But, if I did anything to upset him, then, I would be denied access to go out for another week. Sometimes, he started this by keeping malice with me and leaving me at home alone whenever he was supposed to be home. It was a nightmare for me. I could not use the phone when he was home. I would have to wait until he left for work or went out. But the moment I heard the car pulling up in front of the house or the car garage door opening, I would quickly hang up, otherwise, if he caught me on the phone, it would be another round of punishment.

The one person that I spoke with the most was my aunt who used to live in New York. At this time, she had relocated to Pennsylvania with her family and each time I was on the phone with her and would have to hang up because Tade had come home, she would get upset. I could not tell her that my going out privilege would be suspended if I was caught talking with her on the phone. He would assume that I was talking about and reporting him. He would be upset. And, because, I had not gone out in two, sometimes three weeks, I would try to ensure I did not give him an excuse to deny me that 'treat.'

There were days, I had to peep through the window to see another day break. I was a prisoner in my own home. I delivered our son through an emergency C-section in November 2006. I had dilated up to seven centimeters but was bleeding profusely which was not normal. The baby's heart rate had also dropped. Without hesitation, my midwife summoned the surgeon, and I was immediately prepped for an emergency C-section. It was suspected that the placenta had detached from the uterus thereby obstructing the baby's ability to breath. I spent five days in the hospital, and during this time, Tade was only known as a friend, because I must not tell anyone that he was the father, otherwise, I would be in trouble. Even at birth, Tade was not adjudicated the baby's father and he would not add the child to his medical insurance. I had to apply for medical assistance for our son. I was discharged to go home. However, because of the hardship I had suffered in the hands of my husband during the pregnancy, I requested a birth control shot. I did not want to have another child with him. And, since I had no choice but to give him sex whenever he wanted it, I had to protect myself from getting pregnant.

When we were leaving the hospital, I was cautioned against going up and down the stairs because of the incisions from the C-section; this could cause it to tear.

When we got home, I had to go against the doctor's advice. My bedroom was upstairs and the kitchen – downstairs; but, in order not to die of hunger, I trotted up and down the stairs to fend food for myself, as Tade would not bring me food in the bedroom. Two days after we arrived home, I had asked Tade to prepare a corn meal for me. I needed the liquid food to be able to help my breast milk flow to feed the baby but he would not prepare the food. He abandoned the baby and me in the bedroom and went to chat with his friend in the living room downstairs. I had to call the house phone before he responded, as he would not answer his cell phone when I called him.

By the time he decided to bring the food, I had lost my appetite and could not eat anymore. The trips to and fro the kitchen and bedroom was very strenuous for me because of the pain I was having with the incision. I had to sit using my buttocks to slide on the stairs whenever I did not have enough strength, to hold my belly with one hand and the other on the railings to make the trips. I would also crawl on my knees to get back to the bedroom. It took me 10 to 20 minutes, sometimes, to do this. I was very weak. I suffered and cried but there was nobody I could call for help. I did not know who to talk to and I did not know there was help out there. He pretended to be taking care of us whenever those who are not his close friends were around.

Because he disrespected me in the presence of his friends, they did not respect me either.

I lost my self-esteem because he was always calling Nigerian journalists dummies whenever we had visitors and they were discussing the media. I had at a point asked why he was doing that but he did not give me an answer. I did not know it was part of his strategy to further control me and make me feel worthless. He complained whenever I made contribution to an open discussion among other people. It got to the point that I did not talk much whenever we were with people. I did not want him to be angry with me. I just watched and listened whenever we were among other people with little or no contribution to whatever was being discussed. I did not have friends. I only talked to my clients and it was very limited. I did not tell them what was wrong in the house. Those who suspected did not start any discussion with me, because they did not see me trying to open up to them.

Even the Public Health nurse, Lori, who came to the house to visit during my pregnancy, and after the birth of the baby, could not get me to open up. She would constantly ask if I was depressed but I told her that I was not. There were many times that I wanted to say something to her but fear would not let me. Tade had instilled it in my head over and over that if I said anything to anybody, he would make sure that I was deported. And, at this point, I could not take that chance for the sake of my son.

There were days I would stand before the mirror and stare at the person looking back at me, but I did not recognize her. I would touch my face and ask myself…

…"who are you?"

But the answer eluded me. That was when I lost touch with myself. I didn't know that I was depressed.

Chapter 8

He Neglects His Child

I became more sad and tormented when I saw how Tade maltreated our son, Samuel. I can count on one hand how many times he had ever held his son in his arms. Whenever the baby was crying, I would have to leave whatever I was doing to pick him up. His father just turned a deaf ear to the helpless baby's cries. He complained that I was spoiling the baby by attending to his cries.

I had to go back to braiding hair in less than one month after giving birth. It was even harder on me - I had to tie the baby on my back while I worked, sometimes for 12, or more hours a day. I did this while Tade was sleeping, watching TV or chatting online with his concubines. Other times, he was watching pornography online. I did not know until I caught him on pornography website when we were preparing for church one Sunday morning.

We did not circumcise our son. It was against our religion and a taboo in our culture to have our male child uncircumcised, yet, Tade did not care. He used us to file his tax return in 2006 but refused to give us a dime. When I advised that he should use part of the refund to circumcise our son, he was angry with me and reported me to Uncle Thomas, who called to harass me. I became helpless when nobody would listen to me. It was heart breaking for me to see Tade neglect our child whenever the little boy wanted acknowledgement or attention from his father.

On one occasion, I was cleaning the bathroom in the master's bedroom and I put Samuel by the door to keep him out of the dirt. He began to cry and Tade came into the room. When Samuel saw his father, he crawled up to him, but he was ignored completely. Tade just took something from the room and left. Samuel crawled after his father in pursuit of getting his attention, but Tade continued to ignore him, so the child came back to the bathroom door crying. I saw the hurt in my son's eyes and it cut through my heart like a knife. I was hurt too but was helpless.

He complained that Samuel and I had slept for eight hours while he was working. So, he did not want us to bother him. And, whenever I complained that he didn't help me with the baby, he left us at home without telling where he was going. Whenever I called his phone, he ignored my calls or switch off his phone.

During the summer months, I dare not turn the air-conditioner on. This was not allowed in his house. Tade refused to buy summer clothes for the baby. He had to wear winter clothes during the hot summer, which resulted in him having heat rash all over his body. One of my clients who had suspected that something was wrong saw the heat rash on his body and the winter clothing that he was wearing. She took us to Wal-Mart in Brooklyn Park at 12am to get him some clothes. When the winter began to approach and it was getting cold, we could not turn on the heater. Whenever I turned on the heater, Tade quickly turned it off. Again, he refused to buy winter clothes for his son. I had to call his cousin, Sean, to help beg him to buy clothes for the baby. I waited and when I did not see Tade buying any clothes, I had to call my sick father to help me call Tade's families in Nigeria, to please, beg him to buy winter clothes for his child. I did not want the baby to contract Pneumonia. It was sad enough that I was being maltreated, but, it was more sickening for me to see our child suffer hardship at the hands of his own father. Tade was upset that I called my father and his family to beg him to buy clothes for his child.

Meanwhile, my father had been sick since I left Nigeria. My Uncle, Tony called me one Sunday afternoon to ask if I knew my father was sick. When I called my father, he confirmed that he had been sick but did not want me to worry, especially, after I had told him that Tade was not treating me well. He did not know the extent to which I was being maltreated. I too did not want him to worry about me, so I did not give too much detail. He consoled me and advised that I should be patient, thinking it was just a spousal misunderstanding. When the situation grew worse, I could no longer afford to buy phone cards to call my sick father, let alone send money to him for medication.

Tade, who did not provide for his son, would also not protect him. A kid's modeling agency, Main Kids, contacted us through a letter that it found out about our child. They explained in the letter that they would be interested in using our child for modeling children's products. After reading the letter, I told Tade and he agreed that we should contact the agency. We were given an appointment to take our baby in for evaluation and signing of a contract. At the appointment, the agency's staff member who attended to us told us that they model for Huggies, Parents Magazine and some other companies with children's products.

He also told us how our son would be paid by the hour. According to him, whatever money our son made would be used to open an education account that would help towards his college fund. As someone who believes in education, I bought the idea. My husband showed excitement too. The crux, however, was that we would have to sign up with $599. We were given the opportunity to pay it by installments with a first deposit of $250. Tade said he did not have money. We agreed that I would withdraw the down payment from Samuel's savings account. Samuel had a savings account with TCF bank. I wrote three checks (the installment was in three and they needed the three checks written before we left their office) from my account and gave to the agency staff member. I transferred money from Samuel's account into mine but there was not enough fund in his account. Tade was not interested in how the rest was going to be paid. I had to struggle to braid hair in order to make the rest of the payments with the little I was able to keep back from my 'pimp.'

We had also taken him for photo shots for the same program and paid $20 that I provided. After two month that I did not hear from the agency, I decided to call. There were always no responses whenever I called. I kept leaving messages until the photography company wrote us a letter. In the letter, we were made to understand that the photography company does not have any kind of affiliation with Main Kids. Then, I knew that we had been scammed. I however received the shock of my life to see Tade happy that his child was duped. He said:

"Good for you two. You have been scammed."

I never imagined that a father, who was supposed to be protective of his child, would be happy that someone else had taken advantage of him.

Tade would go to work and not return home at the usual time. Whenever I asked what the matter was, he claimed that he was at work doing over-time. He had told me they would not allow night workers to work more than one hour over-time in the morning, because they had worked without sleeping. There were times he would not be at home, sometimes, for more than four hours. Like any concerned wife, who cares about her husband, I would be worried and would call his cell phone. When he would not answer, I would call his office to be sure everything was fine, as his job was very risky. When he returned home, he would be upset that I called his office.

In April 2007, I went to California with Samuel to spend two weeks with Uncle Tony and his family. When my uncle picked us up at the airport, he was shocked to see my frail body. He could not believe that this was his niece, who came from Nigeria not too long ago. He called Tade to find out what was wrong, but as usual, Tade told all kinds of lies against me. He told my uncle that I cursed members of his family, disrespected, threw things and hissed at his friends. He also told him that I don't heed to his "gentlemanly" advice, rather, I would take other people's suggestions. (I don't know which people when I was isolated from people). He denied ever threatening me with immigration or police and he promised to document our marriage so that he could file the petition to change my status.

My uncle believed him because he displayed one of his cunning tactics. He called us twice a day, every single day, for the two weeks that we spent in California to deceive my uncle. But when we returned home, it was the same old story. We took an overnight flight to Minneapolis from Los Angeles. When we arrived at the MSP International Airport, Tade was not there to pick us up. I had to wake him up by calling the house phone for him to pick us at the airport.

I waited for more than one hour with Samuel who was only five months old. When he eventually picked us up, you would not believe that this was the same man that called us twice a day, while we were in California. He did not say a word to me throughout the 45 minute drive home from the airport. That night, he left for work without asking how our trip went. He came back from work the next morning, and all Tade wanted was sex. I was disgusted and turned off by him, but what choice did I have but to give it to him, otherwise, there would be no rest for me. There was no love felt from him, he just jumped on me like a dog in heat. Within two minutes, it was over. He got up and left without any regards for me and my needs. I felt like I was less than a woman, I felt used.

My uncle called to find out how things were going but I told him things were not going fine. I told him that Tade would not speak to me and that all he wanted was sex. Tade had reported me to Uncle Thomas and Aunt Nancy that I was not giving him sex. They would call to harass me that I was not giving my husband enough sex. They accused me of behaving like an American woman. All my complaints to them about Tade's unruly attitude towards me and our son fell on deaf ears. One of his friends, who lived in Texas, called one day, when we had a misunderstanding. He accused me of not giving my husband enough sex. He even asked:

"So, how many times have you given your husband sex this week."

I felt humiliated and dejected that his friends had to call, to accuse me of denying my husband sex. Even, when I was sick, I had to give him sex. Sometimes, I would bleed for days to the extent that, I would have to use pads, because of the roughness and forcefulness that he used to have sex with me. There was no love making or foreplay to arouse me for the moment. My vagina would be dry and when he thrusts his penis into my vagina, it would burn like pepper in the eye.

I could not go to the hospital because I did not have medical insurance. I could neither have reported it to the police. I did not know that I could report the crime because

I was undocumented. He had always threatened that I would be in trouble. Sometimes, I would be on my feet with Samuel strapped to my back, braiding hair for up to 14 hours without any help whatsoever from Tade. The time that I was supposed to relax and rest, was when he would come to the room for sex. He had isolated Samuel and me in our master bedroom and moved to the guest room to sleep. He only came into our room for sex, and whenever he was finished, he went back to the guest room.

One night, in October 2007, I was not feeling well and was already in bed. All of a sudden, Tade was on the bed demanding sex. I told him I was not feeling well and left to use the bathroom. In the bathroom, I felt dizzy and had to lie down on the floor. Few minutes later, Tade came into the bathroom and saw me on the floor. Without asking what was wrong, he grabbed my hand painfully and dragged me back into the bedroom. He pushed me onto the bed, pulled up my night gown and raped me. I was afraid and helpless. I muttered to him that I was not feeling fine and begged him to stop. My pleadings just fell on deaf ears, as he continued to assault me. When he was finished, he abandoned me in our bedroom and went back to the guest room.

I was so weak. I could not stand up to even go to the bathroom to clean myself up. I fell asleep crying and when I woke up in the morning, I found blood stain on the sheets, my husband had hurt me again. I could not keep it to myself anymore; I felt like I was going crazy and had to talk to someone. I called my aunty when Tade was not at home to tell what had happened, and what I was going through. She advised me to go to the hospital. I did not have medical insurance, so I could not go. Moreover, there was no means of transportation for me to go out of the house, except I was being given a ride by a client.

I also told Uncle Thomas, who only said, silently: "If you know you are not feeling fine just tell him." But I told him I was sick and he would not listen. He only wanted to satisfy his sexual urge. It hurt me to find out that the one I loved had reduced me to a sex material and treated me like an animal.

The burden was too much for me to bear. I had to rely on God for help. I began to pray that God should take me out of the bondage called marriage.

Chapter 9

At The Verge Of Suicide

In July 2007, his cousin, Dokun, whom I referred to as *daddy Germany,* visited us with his wife from Germany. The day before their arrival, I woke up in the morning but Tade was not in the house. I was afraid because I did not know where he went, leaving me alone with the baby. I called his cell phone but got no response. At 2 o'clock in the afternoon he was still not home. He wasn't picking up my calls.

Daddy Germany called to let us know that they were on their way to the airport. I told him that I did not know Tade's whereabouts. He advised me to call his office to find out if he was at work. After I hung up with *daddy Germany,* I called his office. I was told that those who came to work the previous night had left for the day. The person at the other end of the phone, also, made me to understand that, he did not know if Tade was among those that came to work in the morning. I called *daddy Germany* to tell him what I learnt from Tade's office. He had asked me to call, to let him know what was said at the office. He then decided to call Tade's phone, so, I gave him the number. He later called to tell me that Tade picked his phone call and told him that, he was at the store shopping.

When *daddy Germany* arrived with his wife, Kuva on Sunday afternoon, I served the food which I had prepared for them. Tade bought some food stuff in the house because his family member was visiting. After lunch that afternoon, I told *daddy Germany* and his wife my ordeal with Tade. But, after all was said and done, I was asked to kneel down and beg my husband; because, the tradition demands that the wife begs the husband, even, when the husband was wrong. That had always been the case. Uncle Thomas and Aunt Nancy had told me several times to kneel down and beg Tade, rather than, correct him to do the right thing. I would be told that the Bible says, the woman must submit to her husband. Aunt Nancy told me that I did not have the right to question my husband, as I had to be submissive. And, that was part of how they used the faith to deceive me.

I was unhappy and by the next day, *daddy Germany* began to blame me. Tade had told a lot of lies against me; I thought that nobody would hear me but God, so I went to the bathroom with my Bible. Samuel was tied to my back sleeping. He had become used to sleeping on my back. I took care of him like a single parent, despite the fact that his father lived with us in the home. I locked the bathroom door behind me because Tade was in the bedroom sleeping. He had moved into our room when *daddy Germany* came with Kuva.

I knelt down in front of the toilet bowl to pray. I began to cry as I prayed. I felt like my world had crumbled under my feet. Hopelessness overshadowed me and before I knew it, I lost control and began to hit my head on the toilet bowl. Tade, *daddy Germany* and Kuva ran to the door to break it open and I heard *daddy Germany* tell Kuva...,

"...take the baby."

The baby was taken from my back unharmed and still sleeping. Then Kuva said:

"She went to pray, see her Bible."

I was traumatized. I thought only death would take me out of the hardship that I had been suffering, especially, when I was being blamed and Tade encouraged to keep maltreating me. I became even more scared when *daddy Germany* said:

"We would hate your child when you die."

There and then, I was determined to strive to live in order to protect Samuel from ill-treatment, not only from his father, but also from Tade's relatives. I had suffered too much hardship with him for him to be maltreated by his relations after my demise.

Daddy Germany ordered me to kneel down to beg Tade again. I did; for the sake of my life and that of Samuel. Tade had complained that I opened a bank account. It had gotten to the point where I was tired of Tade's extortion and with the help of one of my clients, who worked with Wells Fargo bank, I opened another account. I also sold Avon Products on the side to make additional income. He told his cousin that he did not approve of me selling Avon Products. His cousin had the gall to instruct me that I should desist from selling Avon products. Being in the position that I was, I had no choice but to promise to abide by their rules and regulations. I had nowhere to go; neither did I know that there was help out there, so I obeyed the rules of my slave master and his supporters.

I also found out that Tade was communicating with another woman in Florida. This came to light when I received our cell phone bill and was glancing through to see how much we owed. There were numerous calls to the same number in Florida. The strange thing was the hours which the calls were made, and the duration of the calls. Later on, I found out that it was my colleague's sister, Josephine. She had moved to Florida with her children.

When I confronted Tade about it, trying to find out what business he and Josephine were in, and why he was calling her, especially, at those strange hours, he only got upset at me. Our cell phone bill monthly, was about $70 but

Tade collected $100 from me. Yet, he complained that I was using free phone in America. He had also brought some of Josephine's belongings, including clothing, shoes and jewelry into our home without my knowledge.

About the end of August, Uncle Thomas visited us. He had come to attend a wedding in Chicago and decided to pass through Minnesota for a visit. During his visit, he kept asking me if I was okay, because, even a blind man could see that I was not looking healthy. He advised me to go to the hospital, but I did not have health insurance. I became ineligible for medical assistance after the birth of the baby.

After seeing how Uncle Thomas acted with concern towards me, I decided to tell him what I was going through with Tade and he said he would talk to him. Later on, Uncle Thomas told me that during their trip to Chicago, he and Tade had a discussion. Tade told him that he was maltreating me on purpose because he was not in love with me anymore.

Uncle Thomas said he asked Tade:

"What if she dies?"

But, Tade did not say anything. I became more afraid at that statement. The only conclusion that I could come to was that Tade wanted me dead. Since he could not kill me the traditional ways, his best attempt was to stress me to death. That way, he could walk away from the law a free man.

Chapter 10

I Did Not Want To Go To Jail

In September 2007, Tade registered a business in his name for me to be braiding hair outside the home. He said that he would change it to my name as soon as he filed my immigration petition. We rented a shop in Anoka, about eight minutes from Ramsey where we lived. Little did I know that, this was just an attempt to make me spend the little proceeds from the hair venture on shop expenses. He was not happy that I had opened a bank account. Even though, he promised to help me with payments, I was left alone to sort things out. I was alone by myself with God and my child as my only consolation.

When I received the shop's telephone bill, it was more thanI expected but when I told him about it, his only comment was:

"Welcome to America."

I was at the shop working with the baby strapped to my back, while Tade was at home sleeping or watching porn. Other times, he went to hang out with his friends. It got to a point that he stopped taking us to the shop. I relied on taking a taxi, which cost $15 for a one-way trip, or beg my clients to give me ride, otherwise, I stayed at home.

We did not live on a bus route. I did not know how the mass transit operated because I had been isolated for two years. At that time too, he had stopped buying food in the house. He would go to Cub Foods to buy four chicken wings and drumsticks to cook and eat. Whatever he did not eat or take to work was what I would sneak into the kitchen to eat in order for me and the baby not to die of hunger. The baby was mostly breastfeeding. He would take little rice cereal with Enfamil sometimes. We suffered hunger in the land of plenty.

There was a time when there was no toothpaste in the house, so, I cut the plastic of the toothpaste container open to get the little that was left in order to brush my teeth. Tade also took from the cut container to help finish it faster. One of my clients, who was always willing help bought me toothpaste when I told her that there was none in the house, and that, my husband would not buy toothpaste for us. After I put the new toothpaste in the bathroom, Tade brought out new toothpaste showing that he had bought toothpaste but did not want me to use it.

On Labor Day, I woke up around 5am with Samuel running a high temperature. I gave him a bath but the temperature did not subside. I went to Tade in the guest room, where he was sleeping to ask him to take us to the Emergency Room. He did not respond to me until I told him that I would call the ambulance to take us to the hospital.   When we reached Mercy hospital in Coon Rapids and the baby was examined, it was found that he had an ear infection. We were discharged after treatment and told to watch his temperature. We were told that if it did not return to normal, we should come back to the Emergency Room. However, as soon as we got home, Tade's phone rang and it was Josephine on the other side of the line. When he finished talking to her on the phone, he left me with the child without telling me where he was going. I tried to tell him that we needed to keep an eye on the baby as instructed from the hospital because I did not know how to drive in case we needed to go back to the hospital. He was upset and left.

I called Aunt Nancy to tell her, thinking she would be able to call and prevail upon him to help keep an eye on the sick child. I was wrong. Her response was that, I should go to Tade and kneel down to beg. I obeyed. I did not want my child to die. Luckily, he had returned home early.

On Saturday, October 13, 2007, I woke up in the morning to iron when I overheard Tade telling a woman on the phone:

"Don't worry; I would have done something by Monday. You just get in touch with the lawyer."

I did not know who the woman was. Her voice was not audible enough for me to hear exactly what she was saying at the other end of the line. I had ordered a taxi to take Samuel and I to the shop. I was ready and waiting in the living room for our ride when I saw Tade, who was apparently finished with his phone call came downstairs and went into the kitchen. The kitchen was just an adjacent to the living room.

I realized about a week before then, that my cell phone was not working. Tade was not talking to us, so, I did not bother to ask if he knew why the phone was not working. So, that morning, I gathered the little strength I had left in me, to accost him about the phone. It was then I found out that he had disconnected it to further punish me. Meanwhile I had just paid the bill for both phones. Tade disconnected my phone so that I would be unable to make or receive calls, including long distant calls whenever I was at the shop. He knew that this was how I communicated with my clients, but he didn't care. He also did not want me to see the call details made to his girlfriends.

As we were arguing, I told him I would go and check his cell phone call record to see the woman he was talking with that morning. I went upstairs to check his phone and found that the last number on the call record was a 1-800 number. Still, I did not know who the person was. I kept the phone back. He had followed me but I reached the phone before him. When I got back downstairs, a taxi was waiting at the front of the house. I picked Samuel and left. I did not know that Tade had followed me outside. I was strapping the car seat at the back of the taxi when the taxi driver said:

"That man is talking to you."

I looked back and saw Tade walked back into the house. The taxi driver asked what was wrong, but I told him not to worry. He was, however, adamant and told me he heard Tade said:

"I would show you, you would see."

But I told him to just take us to the shop. As we left, we saw a police car drove passed us. We went a little further, and another police car drove passed. Then the taxi driver advised me to go back home. He said that he was sure of what he heard Tade said.

I did not see my husband calling the police. We only had an argument. However, I heeded to the taxi driver's advice and went back home. When I got to the house, two police officers were there. The taxi driver was right. I greeted them and they asked if I was Bukola. I said...

... "yes."

They asked me to tell them what happened but I was too afraid. I could not tell them the hardship that I had been suffering at the hands of Tade. I told them that Tade was abusing me without giving many details. I told them, also, that he was not taking care of the child.

The police officers were both male and female. The male officer asked where I was going, and, I told him I was going to the shop. He told me to go and I left. I had told the taxi driver to wait for me outside. He took me to the shop. I went to the shop crying and dejected because I did not know what to do or where to go. I did not even know what lies Tade had told the police. The taxi driver encouraged me to go to the shelter or resolve the issue with my husband, but he had no clue what I was actually suffering.

At the shop, I called one of my clients to help me call Uncle Thomas and ask him to call me on the shop phone. Remember, I did not have long distance service. Uncle Thomas called along with his wife. They both blamed me. They even prayed a prayer of forgiveness for me. Aunt Nancy asked if I wanted to go back to Nigeria by being deported. Tade had been telling them that he was going to make sure that I was deported. I found this out when some other people he had told, made me to understand that he was threatening to put me in trouble with the law. He was going around telling people:

"I will make sure she's deported."

I was frustrated. I asked Aunt Nancy if her husband was abusing her and she could not respond. Then Uncle

Thomas said he heard me asking his wife if he was abusing her. He said he would talk to Tade to allow us into the house, as I had nowhere else to go.

That evening, one of my clients gave us a ride back to the house. Even though, the taxi driver suggested the shelter, I did not know where shelters were or how to get there. I went back to the house but I was afraid for the safety of my child and I. When I got home that night, I saw Tade's phone charger. It was broken and kept on the kitchen counter. My fear grew worse. I knew that he had broken it so he could have evidence against me for the police. I did not know what to do, where to go or who to turn to, so I turned to the only person I knew could get me out of the hell house. I turned to God and began to pray as I used to do. I took my Bible and turned to the book of Esther Chapter 5. I used the story of Esther and the Jews to pray and ask God for favor to help me out of this predicament.

I made a call to my aunt with the house phone which had long distance calling. I also called Pastor Ola. I had called Pastor Ola earlier in the year to tell him my ordeal and he never supported Tade's abusive behavior. He wrote an email to Tade warning him against maltreating his child and wife. Tade was more upset that I told his friend, who did not agree with his wickedness. He even tried to portray pastor Ola as a bad person to me. He said that he was a drug dealer and someone who controls other people.

On Monday, October 15, however, a client picked me up from home to braid her hair at the shop. When she picked me up, she saw Tade's car sitting outside and said: "Your husband should have brought you to the shop." I began to cry and she asked what happened. After telling her what had happened, she said she knew something was wrong. She had observed that my husband was not taking care of me even when I was pregnant.

She told me she knew I was suffering hunger, and that was why she brought food for me. She was one of those who had brought food to the house for me while I was pregnant. She said:

"But you did not talk, so, I did not say anything. I suspected you were suffering."

She suggested that I should call my doctor but because I did not have medical insurance, I did not have a primary doctor. Then, I remembered that the Public Health Nurse (PHN), Lori visits us at home. I had signed up for the PHN to visit me at home during pregnancy when I went to enroll for Women, Infant and Children (WIC) program. I decided to call Lori. I left a voice message on her phone. Lori returned my call and came to the shop, as I had directed. I told Lori the whole truth. She somehow knew that we were being maltreated. She would ask during her visits if we were fine, but I could not say no. I would tell her that everything was well out of the fear that my husband had instilled in me. I feared death or going to jail for a crime I did not commit. I knew I could be deported but I had to fight for my life and that of my son.

She did not know about the shop until that day. After telling her my story, she said that the house was not safe for me. She referred me to the battered women shelter. She brought out an orange card from her bag that contained telephone numbers of help organizations and resources. She underlined Alexandra House's phone number. She asked me to call immediately which I did. I spoke with one of the advocates who gave me an appointment for 2pm on Tuesday, October 16 and bus direction on how to reach the shelter. I had told her I would come the next day to enable me pick our vital documents from the house.

I went back to the house with the help of one of my clients. I fled from the house on Tuesday, October 16 with Samuel, while Tade was sleeping. Another client who was in Ramsey to fix her car had called to find out if she could give me a ride to the shop. She was not aware that I had a grand plan to "escape from hell house." She took us to the shop and I boarded the bus from the shop to the shelter. I had called the Mass Transit office to find out what bus I needed to board to the shelter's address.

Chapter 11

My Freedom Regained

As I said in earlier chapters, we barely took anything with us to the shelter. We went there, basically, naked. It was at the shelter that we were given clothing. Not long after we got there, my advocate gave me a Salvation Army voucher, which was how I was able to buy winter clothing for Samuel. Like yesterday, I remembered the day we went to the Salvation Army with another resident and her daughter; who was also an infant. I was leisurely walking around the store checking out the merchandise when my heart pounded. I could hear my husband's voice yelling at me:

"Hurry up! Hurry up!! Let's go! Let's go!! You are wasting my time."

Whenever we went to the store, he was always hurrying me. He would stand behind me like a prison warden yelling at me not to waste his time. I would just pick whatever my hand could grab without trying them on as I would be rushing to get out of the store. Sometimes, they would be announcing closing time. I did not know that the stores had fitting rooms. As a consequence, when I got home and tried the clothing on, it would either be too small or big. There were also shoes that I had bought, but never wore. They were not my size. He would not take me to return them. I concluded that my size of clothing was not in American stores. For an instant, my body froze; I quickly turned around to see if I saw him. Then, it hit me like a bolt of lightning; he wasn't here. I was alone with my son. I was free. I heaved a sigh of relief.

The shelter provided me with bus tokens to be able to go to and from the shop. The first time I disembarked from the bus at Hanson Boulevard was a major mile stone for me. There was a Cub Foods store in the vicinity and I had wanted to get some grocery. To ensure that I was not left stranded, I had asked the bus driver when the next bus would arrive. I alighted from the bus at the bus stop with Samuel strapped to my back. I was making my way to the grocery store when it suddenly occurred to me that, I was walking with nobody behind me. I began to look left and right, like an escapee, who had just escaped from prison. Along the way I kept asking myself:

"Is this really me? So, I can walk alone in the land of the free."

Again, I felt relieved. We entered Cub Foods and I picked some items from the WIC voucher we had. We then went to the deli to buy potato wedges and chicken to eat. One downside for me at Alexandra House was that I could not eat the food they served. Being an immigrant from Africa, I was not yet used to American foods.

As I continued to go to the shop, I assured my advocate at Alexandra House that I would be able to pay for the shop expenses. I was advised to change the business name to mine, which I did. I also left a copy of the OFP at the management's office of the shop. That way, if they saw him around, they would call the police to have him arrested. Thank God for the shop. It helped me a lot in regaining my freedom and spending quiet time. I went there, sometimes, not because I had a client, but for the fact that I had a place to go to. Going back and forth to the shop reassured me of my freedom. The shop was also my sanctuary. I went there to listen to Papa, Bishop David Oyedepo's messages. My siblings had sent me some DVDs of his teachings on faith. The messages reassured me of God's omnipotent power. I went further to buy a wall frame with Hebrews 11:1 inscription – "Faith is being sure of what you hope for, and certain of what you do not see." from Burlington Coat factory at Northtown mall.

As time went by, however, I had become so used to riding on the bus that I would refer to it as my limousine. There were many mornings I had to wake up at 4:00am with Samuel to have our bath, and sat him on the potty. I had been potty training him since he was nine months old. I had to get on the bus at 6:00am, in order to be at the shop by 7:00am for an appointment on such days. Though, I had adjusted to my new surroundings, it was not easy. There were mornings when I had to board the bus in minus 40 degrees windshield with several inches of snow on the ground. Samuel was tied to my back and covered with a blanket to keep his face from frost bite. Thank God for Alexandra House that provided Samuel and me with the proper winter attire to shield us from the wicked winter cold. Alexandra House was our home. A place we could leave and return to without being told that we were privileged to have a roof over our head.

Sometimes, when the advocates asked if I was looking for an apartment or have found one before my immigration petition was filed, my response would be: "This is our home."

I was content with the fact that I had a place to lay my head with my son at night. We did not have to sleep outside in the snow. My husband had always told me that I was lucky to have a roof over my head and not sleeping in the snow.

One morning, a lady stopped in an attempt to give us a ride. She had seen me running with the baby on my back trying to get to the bus which was about to leave. Luckily for us, the driver looked towards our direction and saw us coming. He stopped. He had been picking us from that bus stop, so he knew we were coming to ride on the bus. As soon as I got on the bus, he said:

"You are running late this morning."

I replied,

"Yes."

Coming back from the shop to the shelter was another challenge. The last bus leaves at 6pm, so if I did not get to the bus stop on time, I would be left stranded. Calling a taxi was not an option. It was not affordable for me. Many evenings, I ran like no body's business to board the bus, with Samuel strapped to my back as usual. As a result, we lost many of his winter hats. Sometimes too, we were left stranded at the University bus stop where we usually board the bus when leaving from the shelter to the shop. I was at the bus stop one afternoon with Samuel on my back in minus 40 degrees windshield. The bus that we were waiting for passed us by. I called the transit line and I was told the driver did not see us. After calling the transit line a second time to report the same incident, I stopped calling. However, one of the drivers, whom I spoke with, told me that the University bus stop in Blaine was a hidden one for the drivers.

Then I decided to call the mass transit office and advised them to tell their drivers to always look out for passengers at the University bus stop. I might not be the only one who had been left behind at the bus stop. Many times, I was on the bus weeping and just praying that the Holy Spirit console me. I breast fed Samuel for 19 wonderful months. I kept him close to me to feel the warmth of his touch. It felt like life was gradually slipping out of me. He felt it too. He would show his love to me by holding my face with his two little hands and giving me butterfly kisses on my cheek or a hug. This gesture from my son consoled me a lot. I strived to see another day because of him.

Chapter 12

Meeting Shamera: A Blessing In Disguise

I was not making any profit to take care of myself and Samuel. I was not able to work beyond 5:45pm. There were clients that would not mind giving me a ride but I did not want them to know that I was living at the shelter.

However, there was one client, Shamera, whom word cannot express how she has impacted my life. She wanted to do her daughter's hair one evening but could not come until later in the evening. I told her I would not be able to make the appointment because I would not have a ride to go home. She offered to take me home. After we were done and was about to leave, I told her I now live in her area. She asked if my husband and I had moved from Ramsey. I told her:

"No, my son and I."

When we got close to the shelter I told her to leave me at a nearby gas station so that I could get some noodles for Samuel. I told her that I would just be going across the street to get home. She insisted to wait and take me home.

I tried to persuade her that it was not necessary, but she was adamant. It was freezing cold outside and she said she could not leave me to walk in the cold with the baby. With concern in her voice she asked:

"What's going on? Is something wrong?"

Without saying another word, I started crying. She said she knew I was being abused. She said that I was not looking good. She also noted that she witnessed how my husband acted coldly towards me and the baby when she used to come to the house to braid her hair. But she could not ask then because she did not know me well.

For some unexplained reasons, there was just something about her that drew me to her. I told her my story. She began to cry herself to know that another woman could be going through such torture from her husband. To my greatest surprise, she took off her winter jacket and gave it to me. She said:

"It is cold. Minnesota cold is too much for you to be wearing a jacket that is not warm enough. I bought this jacket last year and I am just wearing it for the first time. Please, take it."

I was dumbfounded to have a total stranger clothe me. I thanked her for her gesture. I took the jacket because I did not really have any warm jacked until we were provided with a Salvation Army voucher at Alexandra House. Shamera promised to render whatever help she could to help us survive in our transitional period. And, she did beyond my expectation. She was God sent. She told me I needed a cell phone to be able to reach my clients, and, for them to contact me promptly for appointments too. She purchased a new cell phone under her plan for me and asked me not to pay.

When I insisted to pay a little amount, she agreed that I should pay only $10. She was always trying to help me with everything she could possibly do to run the shop. In order to generate more revenue, she paid for me to have a business sign outside the building of the shop. Gradually, prospective clients began to call the shop number that was on the sign to make hair appointments.

I was encouraged to work till late while Shamera came to pick me up. I told my shelter advocate about her. She agreed that I could stay late at work. In other words, I returned to the shelter after curfew whenever I had to work late.

Shamera also decided to help with Samuel by babysitting him. She worked from home and has a son, Leon. Leon was the same age as Samuel. She said: "Samuel would have a play mate."

It was not easy at first because Samuel cried a lot. He was so used to me that he did not want to go with another person. He was also a little bit demanding. He was a picky

eater. But, Shamera did not mind. She was willing to help.
She told me:

"Don't worry. Samuel would get used to me."

She was right. After some time, Samuel was always excited to go to her house. He got used to her and when he began to talk, he called her mummy but called me Buki. Buki was what he heard them call me at her house.

Since I was not used to the food served at the shelter, Shamera invited me to cook at her house for Samuel and I. She helped us when I purchased a deep freezer at Mennards in Blaine one snowy night. We drove it to the shop in her van. I stored the food I had cooked in small containers to keep in the freezer. We could not take food into the shelter: I had to eat whatever food I had before I returned there. In addition to our Limousine, Shamera became our chauffeur. I could not explain how she was able to cope. She dropped me off and picked me up at appointments, aside from giving me rides to and from the shop, in addition to taking care of her family after work.

She has five children and she was responsible for making sure the children were catered to. She took the two adults among them to and from work too, until, they were able to get their driver's licenses. And, when Shamera was not available, her husband, Liquenda, was there to help. Her eldest daughter also gave us rides several times after obtaining her driver's license. In fact, her family was very helpful to us. Shamera is a life saver. I remembered vividly one night at the shelter when I was feeling like I would pass out the next moment. The only person that came to my mind was Shamera. Because of the love she had shown us, I felt that if I died, there would be someone to take care of Samuel. I called Shamera and told her to pray for me. As if she knew what was wrong, she called me back a few minutes after and read a scriptural verse to me. I felt a burden was lifted off my shoulder and fell asleep immediately. I was surprised to wake up the next morning. I do not remember the scriptural verse right now but I think God used Shamera to keep me alive from that night. It was an experience I could not explain with enough words. I am grateful that God brought her our way, otherwise, it might have been a different story.

Imprisoned: The travails of a trafficked victim

Chapter 13

A Victim Of Crime

At the shelter, I was made to understand that I could be granted legal status to remain in the United States due to my situation. But when it was time to file my immigration petition, there were many obstacles. The main one was that our marriage was not documented. I was referred to an immigration lawyer. She called me and we spoke. She made it clear that she was not my attorney at that point. She was just asking about my case to see if it had merit and to give me advice. She referred me to the Immigrant Law Center in St. Paul. I met with one of their attorneys who told me she was a student lawyer. After telling her my story, she promised to get back to me. But when she called a few days later, I told there was nothing much that could be done about my case. She gave the same excuse that my marriage to my husband was not registered. A wave of hopelessness over shadowed me, and I felt helpless all over again.

One Saturday morning, I related my story to Becki, an advocate at the Alexandra House. I was drawn to her because she has a resemblance with my mother. After talking with her, she told me about Bri, immigration and refugee advocate for Home Free, another battered women's shelter. She said that Bri would be the ideal person to handle my case. Bri worked with immigrant women who had suffered domestic abuse and human trafficking. Becki said she would talk to Bri and give her my contact information. I was at the shop one Friday afternoon when Bri called. She introduced herself to me and then proceeded to ask me questions. I related my predicament to her. She invited me to attend a support group. From this meeting, I would be able to draw strength from other women who had gone through similar situation. That same day, I went to the meeting in Minneapolis. I had to ride three different buses each way to get there in the brutal cold. It wasn't easy but I made it. Immediately Bri saw me, her comment was:

"You look like an abused woman."

Indeed, I was looking haggard; I had been disconnected from myself, and was just struggling to survive the next minute. I met one-on-one with Bri after the support group meetings. Sometimes, it was at her office in Brookdale. She promised to get me a lawyer and told me the required documents to bring to the lawyer. After that day, Bri encouraged me; she always called to check on Samuel and I. Even when she was ill, she still found time to call. I began to attend the support group meetings. I met other women who had suffered the same fate. Some had emerged as survivors with the help they received through the program. I received a lot of courage and strength from the group.

At the shelter, I was referred to seek therapy since I was depressed to the extent that I could not rcognize myself in the mirror. I began to attend the sessions once a week with Kathrine at the Central Center for Family Resources, now Lee Carlson Center for Mental Health and Well Being. It was very therapeutic and helped me beyond what I expected. It was a welcome difference to be able to talk to someone without being judged or blamed just like the shelter and support groups. Kathrine diagnosed me of Post-Traumatic Stress Disorder (PTSD). She said that my experience was as a result of the trauma I had suffered. She added that most women with similar dilemma go deep into depression which resulted in me not being able to recognize myself anymore. She encouraged me to keep my appointments with her to help me get back to normal.

At one of the one-on-one sessions with Bri, I was scheduled for an interview with an immigration lawyer, Salima. She is an immigration legal practitioner in the United States, who worked part-time for Civil Society. She represents victims of human trafficking and domestic abuse and helps them to get legal status after a crime had been committed against them in the United States. She was very patient and attentive as I related my story to her. She told me that I qualified for one, if not all three different kind of visas that are available to abused and trafficked victims. Unknown to me, she said I was indeed, trafficked and abused by my husband, and that, I was a victim of a crime.

A few days later, Salima called bearing good news. She said that Civil Society, a non-profit organization that helps victims of international human trafficking had decided to take my case - meaning that, they would be providing the legal service to file my petition. After several meetings with her, she gave me a list of what would be required to file my petition. Overwhelmed with joy and hope, I wasted no time in gathering the necessary documentation, including: a signed letter from the detective. Detective Klossterman was not available when Laura, my Alexandra House advocate took me to the Anoka Sheriff's office. A colleague, however, signed on his behalf and gave us the first page of his report on the crime committed against me by my husband. I also, had affidavit of support from family and friends who knew about my ordeal. I also needed a police report, so Laura took me to the Ramsey Police Department to make a report. There was a hurdle, however, at the police department that day. Because I did not report during the incident, the police could not take a full report. The police officer that came out to me was one of the two, who had showed up at our house when Tade called the police to make his false allegations. And, I guess, because Tade had made the first complaint, the officer was not interested in hearing me out. Rather, he told me that he was supposed to arrest me the day they came out to the house but he did not. According to him, Tade had told them that I was abusing our son. I felt humiliated rather than protected and began to cry. I said:

"I am the victim but have been taken for the criminal."

Then, he grudgingly said that he would write the fact that I came to the police department to ask him to document that my husband abused me for two years and nothing more. He did and I included the report in my documentation for my lawyer.

I would however like to note at this point that, there is need for law enforcement officers to be aware that perpetrators of human trafficking and domestic abuse always use the law against the victims. Victims, however, do not file reports during incidents because of fear that has been instilled in them by their traffickers or abusers. Please, be patient and be willing to help in order to get the truth of the matter. After gathering all the documents needed, a petition was filed on my behalf to the USCIS.

With anxiety, I waited patiently and prayed that they would approve my petition and grant me legal status to remain in the United States, if not for me, at least for my son.

Shamera invited me to her church in Brooklyn Center for *Friendship Day*. And, after that day, I decided to attend church with her on Sundays. We were in church one Sunday morning when the guest pastor that was invited from another state went on the Podium and said:

"I was praying last night and God told me there is someone here with legal issue. I don't know who, but God said I should let you know that I (God) am in it."

He then asked that those with legal issues to come out and be prayed for. I broke down crying and went forward for prayers. As if the prayers were answered, I received a call from Salima during that same week that a prima facie had been approved for me. My petition was filed on April 11, 2008. Salima had filed two out of the three visas for me, the VAWA (violence against women act) petition, which allow certain battered immigrants to file for immigration relief without the abuser's assistance or knowledge, in order to seek safety and independence from the abuser. And, the prima-facie determination enables victims to have access to public benefits.

Needless to say, I was very nervous as I did not know what to expect at the other end of the phone, especially since USCIS responded so quickly after the

petition was filed. USCIS is known to take time after a
petition has been filed. But to my surprise, exactly six days
after my petition was filed, I was approved for the prima-
facie to enable me have access to public benefits while the
VAWA petition was pending. At that moment, I fell to the
floor, lifted my hands to the heavens and praised my God.
If it had not been for the Lord on my side, I would have died
at the hands of the man who was supposed to be my life
partner. I thanked Salima for her hard work and dedication.
Immediately I ended the call, I ran to the room where
Shamera was sleeping. I was at her house. I jumped on her
bed and screamed like someone who had just won the
lottery.

Salima sent the prima facie to me in the mail at
Alexandra House. As soon as it arrived, I applied for public
assistance. I was given cash and food benefits along with
Samuel. Samuel was on the benefit before me because he
is a United States citizen. We could not pursue child
support for safety reasons. I was able to get health
insurance through medical assistance. The moment I got
my insurance card, I headed to the clinic for a physical
examination.I needed to be sure that I had not contracted a
venereal disease from my husband. I was afraid that I
might have contracted a Sexually Transmitted Disease
(STD) after finding out that he had multiple sex partners.

The advocates at the shelter were happy for me too. I would be able to leave the shelter and live in the comfort of my own home. I was given a list of several transitional and subsidized housing and applied at several. Exactly eight months after the incident with the police at my husband's house, Samuel and I moved to our own apartment in Anoka. It was a transitional house provided by Elim Transitional Housing Program. I had met with Laurel, my would-be case worker, if I was approved. And, after a second meeting with Laurel and Sue, the director of the organization, I was approved and asked to move in. My diagnosis of PTSD enabled me to be qualified for the transitional housing, as well as, my income. I had outlined my short and long term goals for the organization. I had been working on my laid out goals every day to achieve them one after the other. I met with Laurel every week to access our progress and safety. I was always eager to go to support groups and therapy because it helped me in getting my total health. I was also part of a support group for sexually assaulted victims hosted by Judith through the Lee Carlson Center for Mental Health and Well Being. It helped me a great deal to relate, especially, with the opposite sex and to be aware of "wolfs in sheep's clothing," like my husband.

I was also able to go for the written drivers test at the Department of Motor Vehicles (DMV). Little by little,

Shamera taught me how to drive. Before long, I became a pro and was able to purchase my first car within four months. I did this with her help and someone who was like a father to me, Mr. Sheriff. Mr. Sheriff was a family friend who was always encouraging me to be strong to take care of my son after I told him my predicament in 2007. He was not happy about the way my husband maltreated me.

Shamera was a great help indeed. When nobody would offer to help me, Shamera was selfless at ensuring that we were fine. She gave us rides on several occasions even at her inconvenience without complaining. Sometimes, I could see that she was exhausted but she was relentless in her effort to help us.

We lived at the shelter for eight months, sharing a single bunk but I was the happiest shelter resident. They (the shelter advocates) did not know the extent to which my freedom and health was restored through them.

I went to support groups and therapy in minus 40 degrees windshield with my baby on my back and covered with blankets, but I was happy. I was in touch with myself again. I had regained my freedom and did not need to be peeping through the window any more. I went to use the bathroom one day at Alexandra House, and while washing my hands, I looked in the mirror and for the first time since I left my abusive husband, I recognized the person who stared back at me. It was a day of joy for me. I began to tell everyone that I could recognize myself again in the mirror. Kathrine was even happier that the therapy was helping me.

Aside from the groups I attended outside the shelter, I took part in support groups organized by Alexandra House. One was the *Parenting Class*, which was made compulsory for every pregnant woman and mothers residing at the shelter. I learnt a lot at the classes, parenting as a single parent. In fact, it was the host of the group, Wendy, who advised them at the shelter to allow me to continue to potty train Samuel during our stay at the shelter. And, Marie, one of the advocates loaned us a potty. Eventually, I went to my husband's house with Laura and police escort to get our belongings, including Samuel's potty.

Chapter 14

There Is Help Indeed

As things progressed for me, I told my father in hope that he would stop worrying. He was still on his sick bed. I believed sharing good news with him would give him some inner strength in sickness. I suffered hardship that I never envisaged but I am glad to let the world, especially, immigrant women know that there is help. I made it and any woman can make it too.

Bri always said:

"You can get your papers (legal status) without your abusive husband or anyone who has committed a crime against you."

She was right. Now, I have been granted legal status to remain, and authorization to work in the United States. My VAWA petition was not granted, because my marriage to my husband was not registered, and therefore, could not be used for immigration purposes. I was however, granted a U-Visa as a victim of a crime in the United States. The sufferings I went through, along with the evidence presented to the USCIS, proved that my husband had committed a crime against me.

My son's health had deteriorated while we were living with his father, but now, he's a bouncing healthy boy. He never gained up to one pound each month that he was evaluated by health practitioners until we moved to our own home. Moving to our apartment gave him a lot of relief. I could see him looking happier. His face brightened up the first day we moved into our apartment. He ran around and was just looking amazed. It was as if he felt that our hardship was over. And, within four weeks after we began to live there, Samuel gained one pound and four ounces. It was a big deal for me. I was overjoyed that my son's health could improve in such a short period of time. Lori was happy to see Samuel's health improved. She was very happy that she was able to rescue us by referring us to Alexandra House.

After our departure from Alexandra House, Jen became our advocate and began to visit once a month, providing food and basic needs such as toiletries and diapers from the shelter for six months. We also received Christmas gifts from Lori in form of donations from people who adopted us through the county program and Elim Transitional Housing. Jen also brought us gifts for the holiday.

I continued to braid hair and my shop is improving every day. Now, I am working on ideas to make it better to be self-sustainable. I am currently working on establishing a braiding school, to train people on hair braiding, so that, I do not only braid hair but also impart the knowledge of hair braiding into others through training. I determined to survive and take care of Samuel and I. Now, I have peace of mind, especially, since there is nobody molesting us. I am now able to go anywhere I want. I am free from being locked up in the house against my will. I am most grateful and I am encouraging women who might have been trafficked through false marriage or any other form, or are still out there suffering from domestic abuse - whether it is physical, sexual, mental or emotional, to speak out. There is help. This is not to say that there are not men going through abuse or trafficking in the hands of women. I would like to encourage such men to seek help too. The help available covers both men and women. I wake up every day with a new dream of how to make a better life and take care of my child. He also, has come a long way. He used to be withdrawn from people but after we went to the shelter and he was shown love by those who did not know him or relate to him by blood, he began to socialize with other children and people in general.

I would like to emphasize that therapy and support groups helped me. It would help everyone who had gone through such or similar hardship. The main reason I have decided to go public with my story is to let victims of domestic abuse and human trafficking in the United States, as well as other parts of the world, know that there is help. Don't be a statistic. All you need to do is; make a phone call to the police, shelters or any organization that provides help. Those people at the receiving end of the phone are there for you and not against you. They would show you true love as my son and I have been shown. They would provide the necessary assistance to alleviate your sufferings.

Message to the US Government

I want to acknowledge the United States government for the help rendered through the USCIS, by granting me a legal status to remain and work in the US. I am grateful for the opportunity to live again and take care of my son. I would like to urge the government to keep supporting human rights organizations such as: the battered women shelters, Civil Society and other related bodies to help victims of domestic abuse and human trafficking. My prayer is that the government will continue to render support to such organizations, especially, through financial assistance in order to ensure continued safety and freedom in the society. I am a living testimony of such assistance.

I would, however, like to suggest that victims who qualify under U-Visa should be granted, if not full public benefits, at least, health assistance. If it had not been for prima-facie, I might have still been depressed and not be able to tell my story to help others. There is need for such victims to have access to health services to regain their total health.

On behalf of myself, my son and all other victims that were rescued by such assistance, however, I say thank you.

About The Author

Bukola Love Oriola started her career at the age of six in a private-owned pre-school centre in Ajeromi Local Government Area of Lagos State, Nigeria, where she learnt to write alphabets and numbers.

She was born to Adesola and Adewunmi Oriola in 1976 at Ajeromi. Bukola attended African Church Primary School, Mosan, Ipaja in 1983. In 1995, she finished her secondary education, and obtained a degree in Applied Science, Mass Communication from The Polytechnic, Ibadan, Oyo State.

In 2000, she joined Common Interest Communications Nigeria Limited, publishers of National Interest Newspapers as an Industrial Attachment Trainee few months after her degree. She was placed on the proof reading desk for some months, after which she was made a reporter, responsible for the education desk. Reporting became a hobby as she finds pleasure investigating or sourcing stories. Aside from that, she enjoyed the education beat that helps her sharpen her intellectual capabilities.

On March 1, 2003, she was employed by Century Media Limited, publishers of NewAge Newspaper to cover the education beat. Aside from generating news stories, Bukola generated revenue for Century Media Nigeria Limited through advertisements. At NewAge, she bagged a meritorious award from the National Association of Nigerian Students (NANS), Zone D, for writing human-interest stories. She also received a consolation prize (a certificate and mini tape recorder) in the "2003 Bournvita Reporter Award" from Cadbury Nigeria Plc, one of the leading beverage companies in Nigeria. She, however, emerged national winner of the same award in 2005 having exposed the examination malpractice that occurred between students and invigilators in the 2004 West African Secondary School Certificate examination (WASSCE) in an investigative report she had written and was published in NewAge Newspapers.

Meanwhile, Bukola had enjoyed a scholarship of the German government in 2004 to study Multimedia and Online Journalism at the International Institute for Journalism (IIJ), Berlin, Germany. The program, which deepened her journalistic understanding of online journalism focused on the technical features of the medium, Internet, amongst others. She also learnt how to write and produce stories for the web, as she was introduced to Photoshop and Dreamweaver and to different Content Management Systems (CMS). At the final stage of the program, Bukola together with her colleagues produced her own website. Aside from the general news and feature stories she wrote for the NewAge Newspaper, Bukola published a *career guide* column on the education page, to help prospective undergraduates choose the right discipline and institutions in Nigeria.

Presently, Bukola freelances for print and online media. She is a contributing writer for African News Journal, Minnesota. She gives public presentations to help other victims of domestic abuse and human trafficking victim by telling her personal story. She had presented at the Winona State University, Minnesota State Social Service expo in Bloomington and conference at Moorehead, press conference at the Minnesota State Capitol, Health Partners Clinic, Minneapolis and among other small groups such as the Sisters of St. Catherine's, St. Paul, Minnesota, among others. For her courage, she was honored with the 2009 Change Maker's Award by the Minnesota Women's Press.

In addition, she bagged a Runner-Up Award, presented by the North Metro TV, Blain, Minnesota for her enthusiasm as an Independent Producer. She produces two shows – The Bukola Braiding Show and Imprisoned Show.

She also owns a braiding business to earn a living and find her footing to support herself and son. She is working on imparting the knowledge of hair braiding into other people through training. She is presently producing a hair braiding illustrative DVD to help learners master the various braiding styles.

At leisure, she reads, writes, watch movies and spend time with her son. Being an extrovert, she likes travelling and meeting people.

Author's contact:
1928 County Highway 10, 210 Spring Lake Park MN 55432
Phone: 763-433-9454 or email:
bukola@bukolabraiding.com

Need Bukola for a public presentation at your event? Send your request through www.imprisonedshow.com

Help Resources & Crisis Contacts

For anyone who needs help within the United States, please call the national number or any of the numbers listed here and you would be referred to a place close to you.

Department of Health and Human Services

Sponsored, toll-free, 24 hour **NATIONAL HOTLINE: +1-888-373-7888**

Imprisoned Show

www.imprisonedshow.com

info@imprisonedshow.com

Civil Society

www.*civilsocietyhelps*.org

332 Minnesota St # E1436

St Paul, MN 55101-1326

(651) 291-0713

Alexandra House

*www.**alexandrahouse**.org*

10065 3rd St NE

Blaine, MN 55434-9810

(763) 780-2330

Home Free Battered Women's Shelter

*www.**homefree**programs.org*

3405 E Medicine Lake Blvd

Plymouth, MN 55441-2307

(763) 559-4945

Center for Victims of Torture

Minneapolis, MN
612-436-4800
www.cvt.org

World Relief

Richfield, MN
612-798-4332
www.worldreliefmn.org

Youthlink

Minneapolis, MN

612.252.1200

Help resources & crisis phone contacts

www.youthlinkmn.org

International Institute of Minnesota

St. Paul, MN

651-647-0191

www.iimn.org

info@iimn.org

Destination Freedom

www.destinationfreedominc.org

and

Police: 911

Imprisoned: The travails of a trafficked victim

Identifying International Human Trafficking Victimization in Bukola's Story

–Linda Miller, Executive Director, Civil Society

Evidence of International Human Trafficking under the Trafficking Victim Protection Act, As Amended, 2008

Here as a result of "force, fraud, or coercion"

- She came legally, but remained here as a result of fraud

- Promised that K-visa (spousal visa) would be obtained for her

- Promised love, marriage, life together

- Assured the trafficker wanted children

- Promised he would see that she would become legal in the U.S.

- Legal status used as a threat/promise

- Documents kept in possession of trafficker

- Requirements of K-visa used as a threat/promise

- Use of threat of deportation, jail, lack of status

- Use of threat of arrest, jail, deportation, leaving child in hands of trafficker

- Use of demeaning, dehumanizing actions to cause extreme depression, hopelessness, inability to care for her own safety

- Use of shame with relatives – "coercion"

- Isolation – physically, psychologically, limitations of contact with others (taking her to store just when store was closing), limiting her pregnancy, wellness health care

- Punishments and humiliation; use of power/control

- Use of barriers (lack of knowledge of help availability and lack of understanding of criminal law) to isolate victim

- Inhumane treatment

- Child neglected, hungry, psychologically and physically stressed by dehumanizing treatment of Bukola and stressful conditions

- Use of cultural norms in country of origin as part of "force, fraud, or coercion"

Evidence of Labor Trafficking

- Subjection to labor without pay

- Work under inhumane circumstances (on feet all day when pregnant, with child on her back after the delivery of the baby, long hours)
- Use of labor, labor sold, money taken and kept
- No legal documentation of work, no compliance with State and Federal regulations
- No contribution to social security fund
-